BY SWORD, BY RIGHT

the scott appleton short fiction collection

SCOTT APPLETON

FLAMING PEN PRESS

By Sword, By Right
Copyright © 2010 by Scott Appleton
Flaming Pen Press
Canterbury, CT

All rights reserved. Except for brief quotations in printed reviews,
no part of this publication may be reproduced, stored in a retrieval
system or transmitted in any form or by any means (printed, written,
photocopied, visual electronic, audio, or otherwise)
without the prior permission of the publisher.

By Sword, By Right is an anthology of short fiction pieces by Scott Appleton.
All characters and events in these stories are fictional and any relation
to actual persons or events is purely coincidental.

Cover design by Scott Appleton
Cover images from www.Shutterstock.com
Interior design and typesetting by Katherine Lloyd, www.TheDeskOnline.com
Edited by Kelley Appleton and Hannah Davis

ISBN-13: 978-0-615-41089-0

Printed in United States of America
2010

CONTENTS

Fantasy

    Trapped in Imagination 9

    The Space Sphere: Trapped in Imagination 2 21

    The Trees of Angar Forest............................ 35

    Captain Kanovi: The Fate of the Captain and his First Mate.... 43

    Splintered Sacrifice................................ 45

    The Woodland King................................ 49

    The Prize of Sacrifice 55

Science Fiction

    The World Reborn................................ 67

    Roswell's Cousin.................................. 73

    Comet's Passage 81

    Abacus One 83

Biblical

    Moses and the Lamb 87

    The Faithful Few 91

    The Little Children Come 95

Romance

    Carriage Angel 103

Oddity and Fairy Tales

    The Gates of Bliss................................ 109

    The Contract 117

    The Sorceress and the Mouse 121

For Dad and Mom
By your instruction and correction you gave
my imagination wings.
I love you both beyond words

"Through wisdom is an house built; and by understanding it is established: and by knowledge shall the chambers be filled with precious and pleasant riches. A wise man is strong; yea, a man of knowledge increases strength."
—Proverbs 24:3-5

AUTHOR'S NOTE

If it were not for my fans I would not be writing this introduction. You delved into the fictional worlds I've created since 2009 when I self-published my first novel *Swords of the Six*. Thanks to your enthusiasm I am now under contract for three books through AMG Publishers. But seeing as the first novel will not release until mid-February 2011, I figured I'd better keep you hungry readers fed. I want to always be producing new material for you to sink your minds into.

Therefore I am pleased to deliver this collection of short fiction into your hands.

By Sword, By Right is an honest examination of my writing for the past six years. Unlike other anthologies on the market, this book does not attempt to deliver only my sparkling best. Some of these pieces were written at my career's infancy; such as *The Sorceress and the Mouse*, *The Prize of Sacrifice*, and *The Contract*.

Others, I like to think, are my little gems! These selections include *Moses and the Lamb*, *Trapped in Imagination*, *The Woodland King*, and *The Little Children Come*.

But I am also pleased to present a few works specifically written for this collection. These are *Abacus One*, *The World Reborn*, and *Carriage Angel*.

My love for writing extends into many genres, as this collection shows. Herein you will find fantasy, science fiction, biblical, romance, and fairy tales. Interspersed are bits of poetry—or my attempts at it.

It is my hope that you will read for the pleasure of it. If you are an aspiring author I hope you will be encouraged by some of my early attempts. The evolution of my writing is laid bare on these pages.

In all things I do I pray God will be glorified. Though my efforts are fraught with human imperfection, I pray they encourage the saints and lead sinners to the cross of Christ.

TRAPPED IN IMAGINATION

It was a typical winter day. I sat in my little office. The typewriter was before me. I had positioned it in such a way that I could look out the picture window and see the snow-covered hedges bordering the driveway.

I sighed and focused on the blank page before me. There were only two months left to deadline before my publisher would have my head for not completing the manuscript I'd promised them. I still had fifty thousand words to go—it was not looking good.

My office looked like Al Capone had rifled it. Various unfinished writing projects lay scattered on the floor, collecting dust. Cobwebs adorned the corners and stretched between the log rafters over my head. It was truly a writer's paradise!

I began typing, telling as quickly as possible a mystery that meant little to me—that is, little more than a much-needed paycheck. Oh how I longed for a time years ago when I'd written for the love of it, rather than of necessity! Back then I had used my imagination to explore the impossible and consider the improbable. Back then writing was a passion.

Passion. I needed to regain that aspect of my life; that drive which had made me a success. Where had my imagination gone? Or, where had I left it? I drilled my index fingers into my temples. *Think! Think!* Perhaps the fact that I considered the possibility that I had "left" my imagination suggests that I was not wholly well that day.

Regardless of the reason, I forced myself to think back to the time when I was young and my imagination was vivid. I gave myself over to contemplation for the next hour or more and convinced myself that what I must do was what I used to do: immerse myself in my story, picture things as they would be, and live it all out in my mind.

Thus decided, I thought to myself that not just any subject would do if my experiment were to have a chance of success. A mouse skittered across my desk, stood on its hind legs, and looked at me with its long-whiskered face. Its nose twitched and I wondered why it did not seem afraid.

Suddenly, an idea came to me. I would convince myself that this mouse was a sophisticated little gentleman dressed in a fine black suit, wearing a stovepipe hat, and supporting himself with a black, silver-tipped cane. To my delight, the vision appeared to form before my eyes and soon the "gentleman" mouse was clothed and staring directly into my eyes. His nose still twitched from time to time, but his rodent manners were no longer apparent.

"I beg your pardon?" the gentleman mouse said to me.

My, my! I thought. *This experiment is working better than I had hoped.*

The mouse tapped his cane on the desk and cleared his throat.

It is trying to interact with me? I scratched my hairy chin. It was long overdue for a shave. I directed my attention to the mouse. *What a remarkably realistic rodent—*

"What!"

I jerked in shock as the mouse pointed an accusing finger in my face.

"I am not a rodent." He huffed, stuck his cane under his arm, doffed his hat, and began to walk away. "I am a gentleman of highest birth whose family predates the Constitution."

How delightful! It is insulted. But how can this be? How can something created by my imagination do something that I have not preconceived? I decided to play along with my imaginary mouse friend.

"Forgive me," I said. "I was only thinking to myself and did not consider the pain I would cause you."

He stopped walking away, then returned to face me. "Very well. But from now on guard such thoughts, for in this land they can only serve you evil."

"This land?"

"Jupiter."

I laughed until my sides ached and my eyes watered. *The absurdity of it all: a gentleman mouse living on Jupiter! It seems my imagination is not lost after all.*

The little fellow behaved oddly, in fact it seemed he thought that I was a fool for disbelieving him. He clacked his tongue. "How came you here, Sir?"

I mulled over the question and decided on an equally absurd reply: "A spaceship dropped me here. It seems that the population on Mars has exceeded its limitations, so I was forced to travel out here. Jupiter," I said, "is—after all—far larger than Mars and I was getting tired of Earth."

"Mm hmm." He shook his head. "Lies will get you nowhere in this world, Sir, so I suggest you give me the truth."

Feigning sincerity, I leaned close and whispered in his ear. "Actually, I'm a Martian."

"Nonsense," he said. "Mars was abandoned centuries ago. Besides, you are human and I doubt very much that you have the technology to journey this far into the solar system."

I couldn't believe what I was hearing. This creature was actually disagreeing with me. But how could he? He was a product of my imagination.

The mouse did not continue the conversation. He slid down the desk leg, landed on the floor, and headed for the door leading outside to my patio. I followed, curious to see what else my mind came up with. As I was about to open the door I realized that I could no longer see snow outside my picture window. *Odd*, I thought. Then I opened the door and, with the mouse preceding me, stepped through.

Everything felt, smelled, and sounded real. I was immensely pleased that my experiment was working so well. Soon I would awaken from this daydream, find myself in my study, and my rejuvenated mind would send my fingers flying across the typewriter keys. The manuscript would be finished before the publisher's deadline—and my writing career would be back on track.

A blast of hot air struck me. I gripped my patio railing and looked out upon a vast plain of windblown grasses. A lone tree stood several hundred feet from my position. Its yellowed branches were full of white blossoms. The sky was strange; unlike anything I'd seen before. A layer of clouds high in the atmosphere raced by, streaming into bands of orange, red, and yellow gasses. I could see no sun, no stars, but I perceived that it was daytime.

Jupiter. Very well, Imagination, I can go along with this.

The gentleman mouse, a yellow tree, all on Jupiter—it was a curious combination. The mouse climbed on the railing and waved his hand at the scene. "Told you, didn't I?"

"That you did, Mr. Mouse."

"Please, call me Joe."

I acquiesced. "Joe, I want to see more of this land. Will you give me a tour?"

"Impossible," he said. "Night is coming and I dare not wander in the dark. There are creatures of terrible strength—some of great evil—they hunt in the shadows and none who come upon them live to see another day." He pointed to the yellow tree. "Therein lies your only hope of surviving this night. If you are wise you will come with me and spend the night in the shelter of the tree."

Puffing out my chest and flexing my arm, I rolled up my sleeve and showed him my muscle. "No fear, Joe! I am here."

He would not be persuaded. He insisted on bringing me to the tree. When I reached it, I found that the trunk was far larger than I had believed and a door was cut in its face. This I opened and Joe led me inside. As I entered the tree's trunk and closed its door behind me I shrunk in size until I was no more than two feet tall.

Pixies greeted me, buzzing around me and insisting that I sit down. Here I was, sitting inside a tree. Beside me was a mouse that called himself Joe and pixies were talking to me. It was all so strange, yet somehow it felt right and I had no desire to leave, though I did open the door again to look back at my house. It sat alone, the darkness gathering around it, and I feared for it.

"Joe, why didn't we stay in my house?"

"Only the tree is safe, sir. Do not grieve, your home is not the first to come into this world."

The pixies lit a series of candles along the wall and served me juicy red grapes on a small wooden table. I ate greedily, for my stomach had begun to growl. The grapes were better than any I had tasted.

A disturbance outside caught my ear and I looked to Joe for an explanation.

He swallowed, took his hat off, and held it against his chest. "I am so sorry, sir."

Sorry? I opened the door again. An impenetrable darkness made it impossible to see anything—that is, with the exception of my house; for I had neglected to turn off my office lights. The house was sticking out like a sore thumb and I could hear something big stomping around it.

This is marvelous! So far I've met a talking mouse, dined with pixies inside a tree, and now my mind is adding suspense to the plot. I really should stop this daydream and write my story, for now I have found my imagination.

I closed my eyes and mentally focused on bringing myself out of this dream-like state, but though I persisted for some time I could not wake up. Something smashed into my house, the lights went out, and I could hear the big something tearing up the structure. I rubbed my eyes, pinched my skin—*ouch! That hurt . . . but why? This is only a figment of my imagination.*

I burped and beat my forehead on the wall. Nothing happened, except that I received a few bruises. My environment was getting to me. I had let my imagination run away with me and now I was paying the price. I could not awaken. I was trapped; trapped inside my imagination.

Flames lit the night and my house was consumed by fire. I saw a winged creature outlined against the burning building as it roared to the sky and I trembled in my shoes. *A dragon? Why does all this feel real? What has happened to me? Could it be that I have really come to another world? Am I on Jupiter, or on some world other than Earth? Could it be that I, in my foolishness, have allowed my mind to bridge the gap between my world and this one?*

No longer was this a fun game. It had turned into something different, something sinister. If Joe had been a little larger I would have leaned against his shoulder for comfort. The writer within me feared the unknown, even though I had explored it in books, and now I was face to face with a very ominous unknown. I closed the door.

I opened my eyes the next morning to find the pixies gone. Joe, the gentleman mouse, was snoring in a small cot opposite mine in the round room. *What has happened to me?* I wondered. *If none of this is a dream then it is real. No, that is impossible. I refuse to believe that I am here.*

Try as I might, I could not convince myself that this was all some sort of hallucination. Somehow I really was on Jupiter—or, had the mouse said the land of Jupiter? Where was I? *It's too bad I didn't bring a spaceship!*

A narrow series of steps, carved into the wood on my left, arrested my attention. I made my way to the bottom step and peered around the corner (for the stairway curved out of sight and each step was smaller than the previous one). Joe was still snoring. I glanced back at him then ascended the stairs.

I shrank in size as I proceeded and by the time I reached the top of the stairs I wasn't much larger than a pixie. From where I stood I could see a maze of tangled branches. Paths had been carved in the bark and tiny lanterns were hung from the branches. I followed the broadest path and it led me upward again. Pixies were everywhere. They flitted from branch to branch, chatting on limbs, and cleaning the paths with brooms no larger than twigs. If I had been my normal human size these details would have eluded my eyes, but I was as one of them and saw things as they saw them.

The pixies are fair creatures. As far as I could tell, there were no men and all the women had long, wavy hair. Most of them had let their hair grow until it touched their ankles. Each of them carried a wooden comb and whenever they were sitting still they would brush their hair. I dare say that they were a rather flirtatious lot, for it could not have been coincidence that most of them batted their eyes, fluffed their hair, and smiled when I was near.

They were all equally attractive in their identical yellow dresses and I, flattered by the attention, smiled back and kissed several outstretched hands. But I was more interested in seeing more of the pixie civilization, for it was a most ingenious devising. They had large flower gardens in the tree branches—hanging gardens to be more precise, for the vines held up great basins filled with dirt and in these the pixies had their yards, houses, and gardens.

Having no wings, I could not fly to the hanging gardens so I contented myself with observing from a distance. After a little while, I realized that the pixie whose garden I was staring at was staring back. *She looks different than the others*, I thought. Her hair was long and golden but her face was of an olivine complexion and I couldn't see any wings.

There appeared no way to reach her, until I thought of begging a favor from my pixie admirers. They obliged by grabbing my arms and flying me to the hanging garden. The air was full of perfume-like smells from the wide variety of flowers. The pixie that had caught my interest came to me, a wild look in her eyes.

"Please," she said, "tell me you're here to rescue me."

"Rescue you?" I looked around and lifted my eyebrows. "From this?"

Stamping her bare foot, she turned her back to me. Lo and behold—she had no wings. *Could this be another unwilling prisoner of Jupiter?* I asked myself. *Is she in the same situation as I am?*

"Sir, I do not know who you are," she said. "But I can see as clearly as day that you are not of this world either. I have been here for three years now and in all that time I have never seen another human being. The pixies were kind enough to give me a home and I have been treated well, but I want to go home."

I swallowed hard and hung on her answer to my forthcoming question: "And where is your home?"

"Earth, of course!" she nearly shouted. "I was a writer and one day I became very absorbed in my imaginings. Before I knew what was happening I was stuck here. My house came with me, but the dragons destroyed it within a couple nights and I have no clue as to what I should do to get out of here."

"My house is here too!" I said. "And I came here under similar circumstances." I grabbed her hand and called for some pixies to fly us to the branch trail. "Come with me," I said to my new friend. "I know someone who may be able to help us."

It was then that I realized the pixies were laughing at me and praising each other for capturing me. *Oh my goodness, they mean to keep me here!* There was no way off the hanging garden and the lady whom I had meant to rescue started to cry.

Use your brain, I told myself. *There is a way out of every puzzle.* Though I thought hard I could think of no solution. That is until I overheard a pixie declare that she wanted me to remain unscathed. "Come on!" I ran toward the garden's edge with my companion in tow and jumped off.

The pixies reacted in the manner I'd hoped for. They saved my lady friend and me from certain death and set us on a branch. "What were you thinking? You nearly got us both killed!"

"No, I didn't," I replied.

"Then, wise guy, how did you plan to stop our descent?" She took a fierce stance and I smiled.

I brushed a bit of leaf from my shirt and pointed at the pixies. "They may have wanted to keep us prisoner, but underneath they are not bad little people. I knew that they would not permit us to die."

She seemed satisfied with my answer—at least for the moment—she relaxed and asked me what was the next stage of my plan. I led her to the stairs in the tree and brought her down to the round room at its base. As we neared the stair's base we grew a little taller. Joe was still in the room and his whiskers twitched when he saw my companion.

"Who's this?"

"A friend," I said. "It seems that she too came here without a clue as to why or how. I was hoping you could shed some light on our predicament."

He sat at the table and indicated we were to do the same. Then he told us that he was not sure how we got to this place and that this was not the planet Jupiter. "I did visit that planet once," he said. "Nasty place, similar to here in a few respects."

"Where are we?" I asked.

"Nowhere, and somewhere, as well as everywhere."

I threw my hands in the air. "What is that supposed to mean?"

"Have patience, and I will tell you: You are on a world that exists out of time and therefore cannot be reached in physical space. This is the World of Imagination and only through imagination can transport to this place or out of it be accomplished. We are in the Land of Jupiter. It is a confused place in the World of Imagination, full of terrible creatures at night and lovely ones in the daylight.

"I can tell you little else except that you must leave soon if you are to leave at all, for the longer you stay the less power you will have to convince yourself that you belong in that other time, that other space wherein you were born. Once you believe that you are stuck here there is no going back."

At last, I thought, *there is hope for me!* "Joe," I asked him, "are you saying that if I can convince myself that I don't belong here I will return to my world?"

He nodded his head.

I laughed with relief. "Let's go." But when I stood and put my hand on the door the lady came to mind and I turned to find her with tears streaming down her lovely face. "Didn't you hear?" I said to her.

"All one must do is mentally convince themselves that they are not here! If we return to the place we first were when we came here then we will be able to transport off this World of Imagination."

"Don't you get it?" she asked. "My house was destroyed; I cannot recreate the scene. Besides that—time is against me, for I have been here for a long while."

I looked to Joe for help. "I am sorry," he said. "It would seem she is correct."

The lady wept afresh at this proclamation and I put an arm around her shoulders to comfort her. "Surely there must be a way for you to leave this place, too?"

Her shoulders sagged and I knew she'd given up hope.

I ran my fingers through her hair and knew that I must bring her back, whatever it took. "I will figure a way to come back for you," I said. "Nothing will stand in the way; I will bring you home."

"Really?" she asked. Her sobs lessened and she stood up and kissed me on the cheek. "Then go, my valiant knight, before you are trapped here as well."

Setting my jaw firmly, I followed Joe outside to my house. Parts of it had been ruined, some of it was burning, but the office was still intact. Joe got up on my table and I sat in front of my typewriter.

The view outside was real and my heart ached for the lady. *I didn't even learn her name—*

"Flora," Joe said. "Her name is Flora Livings."

"I don't know how you read my mind, Joe, but thank you."

He shrugged his little shoulders. "One of the pixies whispered that to me." He doffed his stovepipe hat and smiled. "Keep your word to her," he told me. "She is as fair as any pixie and a sight more intelligent." Smoothing his whiskers, he continued. "If you cannot return, you will never forgive yourself for leaving her—"

"That will not happen. I *will* come back for her."

I gripped the table and focused on the conditions back home when I had last been there. The snow on the ground, the clutter of my office, the deadline I needed to meet—all seemed to be in place and I believed that was how it was. But something was missing in the equation: I looked at Joe and recalled how an ordinary mouse had been in his place.

My mind eased and I felt weak. Joe's face lost its intelligent expression. His clothes disappeared (along with his cane) and in his place stood the mouse. It sniffed the air for a moment, and then scurried away. Darkness fell on me and I lost consciousness.

A year has crept by since that strange happening. I finished my book, cleaned my office, and my career is back on track. But something is missing and now I wonder if all that happened was actually real. Is there a World of Imagination where a gentleman mouse named Joe lives in a tree in the land of Jupiter? And did I really promise a Flora Livings that I would rescue her from that world? Perhaps I will never know. But I know for a certainty that I must find out the truth, for—though it may sound absurd—I think I fell in love in the World of Imagination and I think that I have an obligation to return to Jupiter and rescue that beautiful lady.

THE SPACE SPHERE: TRAPPED IN IMAGINATION 2

It was six o' clock, a Friday evening in the dead of New England winter. Jacob's small cabin was already half-buried in snow. It reminded him of cotton candy . . . only a whole lot of it! As if, instead of snowflakes, entire balls of fluffy candy had fallen from the sky, heaping on top of each other until the house was an island in the middle of a cold white sea.

Indoors the stone fireplace burned with winter cheer. Jacob smiled, forcing himself to turn his eyes away from the window that gave him a view of the fresh-falling snow. Ah, he loved winter. The isolation was complete. No one would be disturbing him now.

He dropped into his soft easy chair and crossed his feet on the warm hearthstones. His wool socks were a boyish red but oh so soft, his feet felt lost in them. He'd knitted them himself. Here, far away from social activities and his daily work routine in the city, he liked to draw himself back as far back in time as possible to forget the modernized world of which he was a part.

Here he had no electricity. No television, no radio, no lights. Instead he'd installed oil lanterns in the walls, a wind-up record player stood in the corner of his tiny living room, and instead of action films the wall to his right and the wall to his left were lined with cherry wood bookshelves stocked with the finest edition volumes he could get his hands on.

And for company (for he didn't really care to be completely alone but he did not like dogs or cats) Jacob made a clucking sound with his tongue and a creamy-haired ferret climbed out of its carpet burrow in the corner of the room. Running on all fours, the animal dexterously climbed the chair and curled up in Jacob's lap.

He stroked it, smiling again. "Hello there, Sigmond . . . warm enough in here to take a snooze. What do you think?"

The cabin creaked as the wind howled around it and the fire burned higher.

Jacob closed his eyes and let the steady rise and fall of his pet's breathing lull him to sleep. Only one week, that's all that remained of his vacation time. He pushed the troubling realization out of his mind with the hope that the snowy weather might close him in, giving him a proper excuse to overstay his granted timetable.

That evening he fell asleep and dreamed.

He was standing on a pitted gray rock that twisted like a corkscrew. Around this rock was nothing except the blackness of space and, granted, a few more floating rocks that all seemed to form a high orbit around an enormous planet. Any planet, he knew, would appear large from this proximity. In fact if he had orbited Earth in this manner it would have seemed enormous as well.

No, he decided, this planet was gargantuan . . . like Jupiter. The orange and red clouds whipping around its surface opened only on rare occasions. And when they did all he could see beneath them were more and more clouds traveling equally dizzying speeds, except in the opposite direction.

Never before had he dreamed anything like this.

Just as he was beginning to wonder where his mind was leading him, or rather where this dream was taking him, a peculiar thing happened, though it did not seem as peculiar to him as it might have, because he knew that dreams do not often make sense.

As he stood on that floating rock, or asteroidal moon, a piece of the planet's atmosphere welled up like a bubble. It blew into a perfect sphere of an orange, glassy transparency. Jacob's asteroid seemed to hang motionless in space as the atmosphere bubble separated from the planet, floating toward it against gravity's pull.

When the bubble bounced against the tip of the asteroid, it did not rebound into space as Jacob expected it to. Instead, it dropped onto the asteroid's surface in a soft landing, wedging itself in one of the small craters on the space rock's surface.

Amused, Jacob walked along the asteroid and looked at the bubble. Curiously enough, even though the surface appeared made of a liquid substance, it did not mirror its surroundings. He could not see himself, or the asteroid, or the planet, or even space beyond, reflected in its surface. But he could see *through* it without any difficulty, to the surface of the asteroid under it and the blackness of space behind it.

He reached out and touched it. The bubble's surface felt like jelly, cool. When he dipped his hand through the outer shell it felt warmer inside. In fact, it felt as warm as the room he was even now sleeping in.

The strange dream blinked around him. He blinked. It flashed and faded and he opened his eyes.

Jacob stretched and gently picked up the sleeping ferret, placing it on the seat's cushion. Reaching into the large woodbox beside the fireplace, he picked up two split quarters of log. Lifting them to his face he smelled the seasoned wood, half-closing his eyes with pleasure. He cast the two pieces into the fire, held his hands palms out, letting the heat sear into his fingers.

It was at that moment, when he rubbed his hands together, that he caught a glimpse of the curious object standing in the corner of the room. Why, when he turned to look, it looked rather like the sphere in his dream. But that one had been orange and this one was clear.

He picked up Sigmond and stroked his fur, kneeling in front of the sphere. It seemed non-reflective, like in his dream.

The ferret stirred at that moment, its small black eyes blinked at the sphere as it awakened.

For a long while, Jacob puzzled over the alien object. One thing he knew for certain, this had not been in his cottage before he fell asleep.

Suddenly filled with suspicion he went to the window and looked outside. Even though it was dark he could clearly see that the snow around his house was smooth, unmarked by an intruder's footprints. Yes, the snow was still falling but the clock read quarter after six and the snow was no longer falling thick or fast enough to cover human tracks in that amount of time.

So . . . the sphere hadn't come to him from the outside. Then, from where had it come?

The sky? Oh, but that seemed absurd. Why or how in the world could this *thing* have dropped through his roof?

"Sigmond," he scratched the ferret's tiny head, "what do you think?"

His little friend offered no reply apart from blinking its eyes.

"Hmm," Jacob felt puzzled. He started to walk and turned, intending to look at the sphere again. Something on the floor, a book perhaps, tripped him as he moved. With a startled yell he fell onto, through, and into the sphere, with his ferret still clutched in his hands.

At first he felt as if he was drowning in jelly, then he fell through it and let out a "Yipes!" as he descended through a pale orange sky. The air around him at first burned like oil. As his descent accelerated, the air cooled to a temperature equal to mid-summer. The sky above him made him feel infinitesimal.

He tried to hold his ferret, but in the chaotic plunge Sigmond slipped from his grasp.

A yellow mountain rose beneath him and he prepared to meet his death. He closed his eyes. Then he felt his descent slow to a gentle fall and, as he opened his eyes, he landed in a field of golden grass. His feet touched down lightly in the soft ground and he looked around to find himself standing on the surface of, he tried to guess where he was but he could not, it was most definitely not Earth.

Orange and red clouds raced each other across the sky. Above these clouds he could see only more clouds. Though he tried, he could not see the planet's atmosphere. A gentle breeze blew steadily across the slope of the mountain on which he stood, bending the blades of golden grass. If grass like that grew on Earth it would dazzle the eyes, reflecting the sun's rays, but here the sun did not reach. Instead the clouds glowed, spreading warm light across the planet's surface.

The mountain sloped away from him. The fields of golden grass covered it all the way to its base. Jacob could see trees covering the landscape in that direction, and hills beyond.

He turned around and almost bumped into someone standing behind him, towering above him, the hulk of a very old man. Looking up at the man, Jacob estimated his height approached eight feet. A thick beard filled most of the man's face and drooped all the way from his chin to the ground, even trailing a bit in the golden grass. He held a gnarled wooden staff almost twice his height. In spite of that, the old hulk held his other hand on top of the staff, leaving his arm ridiculously stretched vertical from his shoulder, as if reaching heavenward.

A long sliver of golden grass blade stuck out of the old hulk's mouth and on it he chewed with a bored blankness in his black eyes. He frowned back down at Jacob. "Farseethee, young thing, and nowseethee the Land of Marsooth. It stretcheth ever farther and farthest of all places. Know thee where thou art, young thing?"

"What?" Jacob swallowed as the old hulk took a step toward him that made the ground shake.

"Farseethee and nowseethee the Land of Marsooth," the old hulk repeated. With a long, wrinkled arm he gestured at the land, but his gesture was weak and he dropped his arm back to his side. "Nowseethee and hereseethee where thou stands . . .," he frowned deeper. "What are thee and from where do thee come?"

Jacob was still stunned by the suddenness of his transport from his cabin into this . . . other world. "Where am I?"

"Nowstandthee in the Land of Marsooth."

"This is called Marsooth?" Jacob placed his hands on his sides and looked up at the orange and red clouds vastly beyond his reach. "Am I on some planet? It feels, looks like, a strange dream."

"Seetheehere, young thing," the old hulk barked, "I will not hear thee desecrate me beautiful land. Place of dreams? HA! If this is thy dream then what am I doing here? Nowanswerme, young thing!"

"Uh, yeah," Jacob nervously waggled a finger up at the old hulk's face. "You're not making much sense."

"Whatseethee, whatseethee?" Trembling from his massive head to his enormous bare feet, the old hulk swiped at Jacob with his fist.

And Jacob took off running as fast as his legs could carry him. He was a rather thin man and of ordinary stature, but in that moment he ran with the speed of a gazelle. His socks did not provide his feet with much protection from stones and such as he ran, but thankfully the wool did cushion them a little.

When he exhausted his breath, he sat in the field, glancing behind to be certain the old hulk had not followed him. The oversized man was lying facedown in the field, apparently having tried to pursue Jacob, he'd tripped over his own feet.

Breathing a sigh of relief, Jacob stretched out in the grass and closed his eyes. He missed New England! He envisioned the snow, the cold outdoors and the cozy fire in his cabin . . . what had happened to pull him away from all of that? Ah, it was that sphere, that accursed sphere.

Wait! He sat ramrod straight and smacked himself in the face. What happened to Sigmond? "Oh, no! My poor pet what have I done?"

Just then something touched his shoulder. Turning around, he fell down again. It was his ferret, now grown to the size of a tiger.

Sigmond sniffed at his shirt, his black eyes looking at him, squinting at him. Then his mouth twisted open and his ears twitched. "Jacob?" it asked in a deep bass. "Is it really you?"

For a while, Jacob could not close his mouth enough to reply. Then he stood to his feet, brushed the soil from his black sweatpants. Stroking the ferret's silky side, he swallowed hard. "What's happened?"

"I don't know," Sigmond said. "You tripped over *20,000 Leagues Under the Sea*, we fell into that strange sphere, and now we're here."

"*20,000 Leagues Under the Sea* you say?" Jacob put his hands on his sides. "I thought I shelved that volume."

"You did."

"I don't follow," Jacob frowned.

"Well," Sigmond snaked his long body around the man and nuzzled him gently, "you aren't the only one who likes Jules Verne."

"But you're a ferret—"

"Not just any ferret, Jacob. I am *your* ferret. And, even though I admit to a measure of enjoyment in being able to communicate in this manner, I find both my size and that of this land's inhabitants too disturbing to linger."

"Oh, you met the hulk I assume?"

"Indeed," the ferret shook itself from head to tail.

"Well, if you're all for it," Jacob bit his lip and gazed down the mountain slope, "I say we move on as fast as possible and find a way out of this mess."

"Agreed." As Jacob started to walk, Sigmond held him back with a paw. "I believe that if you climb onto my back we will make better time."

"Fine . . . if you think you can carry me."

"Without a doubt, Master."

The ferret bounded down the slope, eating the distance as fast as any horse could have. When they reached the forest at the mountain's base, they continued on. Sigmond navigated between the trees without difficulty and continued on for several hours without breaking a sweat. At last they came to a house in the forest and stopped to inquire of the owners. But no one seemed to be at home so they continued on.

Braking to a sudden halt in a clearing, Sigmond almost toppled Jacob from his back. A broad moat lay before them, separating them from a most peculiar little castle made of wood. A narrow drawbridge spanned the moat. They crossed it and entered the castle's courtyard.

Jacob slid off of the ferret's back. Together they walked inside, calling timid greetings in the hopes of soliciting a reply from the silent occupants.

"You know, Sigmond," Jacob whispered after they'd passed through several narrow and equally empty corridors and looked into each empty room as they passed, "I really miss home."

"As do I," the ferret assured him.

"Then why do you not return?" As if out of nowhere, a tiny figure appeared on the molding half-way up the corridor wall. It was a mouse, though not an ordinary mouse. It sported a smart black suit, tuxedo-like, and while it leaned on a straight black cane with one arm it held an Abe Lincoln hat in its other. A pair of spectacles even sat upon its nose and its whiskers dropped in a dignified manner.

Sigmond answered the mouse's question before Jacob could collect his wits. "We don't know how to return. Indeed, we don't know how we got here in the first place."

"Ah, an accidental drop-in to the world of Imagination." The mouse twirled its cane and walked along the molding, coming closer. "What are you," it asked Jacob, "a writer, poet, artist, or none of the above?"

"I work at an insurance agency, if that's what you're asking."

"Hmm, curious . . . it is usually the bookish, artist types that end up in this place. Not insurance agents. But you, on the other hand," the mouse twisted shook its head as it looked at Sigmond, "how you came to be here I cannot even guess. Is it not true that in that other world you are incapable of using your imagination? That you are, in a word, soulless?"

"Quite the opposite is true," Sigmond held his head high and showed his teeth. "But in the other world there is an invisible communications barrier between animals and humans. It is insurmountable by all but a very few species. But I have learned to read from my master and to enjoy a good story."

"Intriguing," the mouse said. "Remarkable. I will have to present this find to my esteemed colleagues at the Institute for Imaginative Pursuits.

"Now, as you are no doubt wondering where you are, I will tell you. You are trapped in another dimension. I know because we get your kind dropping in here all the time. I'm afraid most come to stay. Their imaginations are too weak to pull them out of this place and some of them have now grown into dreadful men as old as imagination itself. Hulks of humanity they are, with nothing but fog left in their brains.

"This world is a nightmare for some, a dream for others. Almost everything that anyone has ever imagined is here, in some form or another, in the World of Imagination. Some visit this place in their dreams. Others come here by complete accident, fiddling with the powers of their imagination, unaware that they can be trapped in its clutches."

"I did have a strange dream," Jacob leaned against the wall, crossing his arms. He told the mouse of his dream and of the sphere and how he and the ferret had fallen into it when he found it in the real world.

"You are most fortunate," the gentleman mouse put his tall hat on his head. "Such spheres are rare, but not unheard of." It dropped to the floor and looked up at him. "I can get you back home if you'd like, but it may not be easy."

"You can?" Hardly containing his glee, Jacob slapped Sigmond's back.

The ferret looked up at him, an amused smile playing across its face.

"Of course," the gentleman mouse said. "All we need do is find you another space sphere and throw you in. You'll be returned home in the same manner you came. Please note," mouse held up a scrawny finger, "this method will not work for any other individuals trapped in Imagination. Only those who entered this world via a space sphere can return via a space sphere.

"So," it cautioned, "if you should meet any others trapped in Imagination, do not offer them the same means of escape. They must find their own path, a path in keeping with the manner in which *they* became trapped. These laws govern Imagination and they are indisputable and unbreakable."

Jacob smiled at his ferret and then looked down at the mouse. "All right, where can we find another space sphere?"

"This is crazy!" Jacob was shaking in his socks. Beside him, Sigmond didn't look any happier with the situation than he did.

"I do agree, Master," the ferret said in its deep voice, "but though I see no way to obtain our objective, I also do not wish to stay in this place."

"Well neither do I, but that mouse was crazy to suggest . . . *that*," he peered through the bushes again.

A silver and gray dragon stood at the opposite side of a small meadow. The row of horns running from the crest of its skull to the base of its neck continued to the tip of its tail. It wasn't as large as Jacob'd thought a dragon should be, though the cave it was apparently guarding looked like it could fit a monstrous-sized beast.

Suddenly a horse and rider appeared, rushing at the dragon across the meadow. Dressed in classic, shining armor, the knight yelled as he attacked, lowering his lance to strike the creature.

The dragon sat down, unfazed. It waited until the knight's lance bounced off its scales. As the knight passed by, circling for another attack, the dragon held up its hand and flicked the rider from his mount with one claw. The screaming knight flew through the air over Jacob's head. By the angle of the knight's flight and the speed at which he was moving, Jacob thought it safe to assume the knight would not return. The knight's horse ran away. Jacob could have sworn it was calling out the knight's name.

Sigmond's fur was now standing on end. His black eyes were wide open.

Fighting not to let his fear get the best of him, Jacob walked though the shrubs. He heard Sigmond gasp, "Master, don't do it!"

Jacob marched across the meadow and stood opposite the dragon.

"No, not another one," the dragon rumbled without looking at him. "Come to poke fun at me, as well, have you? Well," it stood, a great chain around its neck rattled as it moved, "come on, slayer."

Following the chain with his eyes, Jacob saw a thick ring of steel binding it to the shelf of stone around the cave entrance in the hill behind it.

"Well?" the dragon seemed to be waiting for him to attack.

"Um, excuse me," Jacob held up his hands. "Don't worry. I'm unarmed, and even if I were," on impulse he made a bow to the dragon. "Even if I were armed I doubt I could kill you."

The dragon cocked its head to one side. "I can't tell if you mean that, or if you are using flattery, or if you are tricking me into lowering my guard."

"I do mean it. I'm not a fighter . . . even if I wanted to I wouldn't know how. And after seeing the way you dealt with the last slayer," Jacob chuckled nervously, "I don't think I'd want to mess with you."

"Well, there's a first for everything," the dragon blew smoke out of its nostrils. "What are you here for, if not to kill me?"

"I was told," Jacob cleared his throat, "that there is a space sphere in this cave . . . I need it."

The dragon started to laugh deep and loud. "And you think I'll just . . . let you through?"

"Well, I was hoping . . . or maybe," he snapped his fingers, "an exchange?"

Sitting back on its haunches, the dragon blew more smoke from its nostrils. "What did you have in mind?"

"What if I freed you?"

"Unlikely," the dragon said. "You admitted that you are not the warrior type and if this chain could be broken by you, don't you think *I* would have broken it by now?"

Jacob frowned. He hadn't thought of that. But he shrugged his shoulders. "It's worth a try . . . if you'll agree to my terms."

The dragon harrumphed and waved a clawed hand at the cave's face. "Very well, but if you attempt to enter the cave without freeing me, I will fill it with flames so hot you will melt in three seconds . . . Consider yourself forewarned."

Three seconds, that chilled Jacob's heart. He swallowed hard and followed the chain to where it attached to the stone. A steel plate held the chain's end ring in place. Feeling around it with his fingers, Jacob almost laughed. The plate was held to the rock with large pins which, if he could slide them out of their respective slots, would free the chain from the stone. The pins were too small for a dragon to manipulate with its claws but perfect for human hands.

It took him no more than half-an-hour to pull the pins loose. When the chain dropped, the dragon smiled at him and waved him toward the cave entrance. "The prize is all yours. Just be careful in there. The space sphere is the property of my captor . . . whose path you should pray you do not cross." With that the dragon stretched its wings and sprang into the air, dragging the chain behind it.

Sigmond emerged from behind the bushes, looking a bit sheepish. Jacob stroked the ferret's soft fur and told it not to worry, they'd soon be home.

And into the cave they went. It was dangerously dark, to the point that they could not see their way more than a few feet at a time. And suddenly a slimy black body slid past them in the darkness and two beady yellow eyes shone at them.

"Run!" Jacob said, making pell-mell for the cave entrance.

They rushed back outside and turned to find a gargantuan King Cobra snake rearing to strike, venom dripping from its fangs. Before Jacob could even consider what to do, he saw Sigmond rush the serpent.

The snake dove for the ferret, but the ferret was quicker. It jumped for the snake's throat and ripped it out with its teeth. As the King Cobra fell, Sigmond wiped his bloodied fur with his paw.

"Now that's what I call impressive," Jacob hugged his pet around the neck.

Sigmond tore one of the serpent's eyes from its head and held it in his teeth. Jacob tried to hide his disgust as they made their way back into the cave. When the darkness closed around them this time, the yellow glow of the snake's eye lit their way.

Deep in the cave, in a round chamber, resting on a steel pedestal, an orange sphere glowed in the darkness. Before jumping into it, Jacob looked down into Sigmond's eyes. "If there is one thing I'll miss from this whole wacky experience, it'd be being able to talk to you."

The ferret smiled. "Do not worry, Master. I much prefer to listen. As long as you promise to keep reading aloud, I'm more than happy to return."

"Deal!" Jacob jumped into the space sphere and it absorbed him with eagerness. He fell through the cold shell, then felt the warmth of his fire greet him, and he landed with perfect precision in his easy chair. An instant later, Sigmond appeared in his lap and curled up. His black eyes blinked up at Jacob as if he'd been there all along.

Jacob reached down to the floor and picked up the book he'd tripped over. *20,000 Leagues Under the Sea*, he read the gold lettering on the cover and opened it with one hand, stroking his ferret with the other. He opened his mouth to read but his eye turned to the corner of the room where the sphere still rested.

He started to consider whether or not to attempt removing it, then decided against it. So long as he was careful not to fall into it again, it could sit there as proof that he had not lost his mind.

"Now, Sigmond," he said, turning to the first chapter, "let's start from the beginning." Five minutes later the book was face down on the chair arm. Jacob was snoring softly and his pet ferret lay asleep in his lap.

THE TREES
OF ANGAR FOREST

Phillip wrapped his arms around the tree's twisting branch and gritted his teeth as the tree tried to throw him off. His body felt like a leaf held to the branch by the barest roots of its stem.

"You are strong, Phillip." The tree's creaking voice interrupted his concentration and the branch Phillip was holding slipped along his sweaty arms. Bits of bark cut into his skin, leaving their marks and riddling him with splinters before he tightened his hold on the tree. "Yes . . . strong indeed," the tree said.

Between heavy breaths Phillip managed to glance back at the oak tree's trunk. "Thanks," he managed. "You're not too weak yourself." The bark parted midway up the trunk into an easy smile and the branch ceased throwing him to and fro. Slowly the branch began lowering him to the cool grass which surrounded the tree's base. When his feet touched ground Phillip loosened his cramped arms and released the branch. "Now what?" he asked.

"Now you tell me what sort of fair maiden has you under her

spell." The branches of the tree stretched to their natural positions some ten feet above Phillip's head and the tree's trunk creaked as it angled slightly toward him.

Wiping the sweat from his brow with his shredded shirt sleeve, Phillip waited as a gentle breeze washed coolly over his body. It felt refreshing but what he really wanted was water.

"Well, Phillip?" the tree said.

"You want me to tell you about my Love?"

A protracted creaking sound seemed to verify Phillip's assessment.

While golden rays of sunlight filtered down through the tree's voluminous branches Phillip stood still and regarded the tree with his tanned brow furrowed. It seemed an odd request for a tree: 'Tell me what sort of fair maiden has you under her spell.' But, then, this was the oldest tree in Angar Forest. Or, at least, it appeared to be. Its trunk was broader and its bark harder than any other. And no one that Phillip had spoken to had any idea when the tree had come to be. Perhaps age played a factor in this tree's interest, though Phillip would have preferred to simply wrestle the thing until it agreed to provide the lumber for his home.

Joel, Nathan, and Edward, friends of his, had all wrested smaller trees so that they could build themselves houses to which they could bring their brides. But all three of them had returned with lumber unfit for building and the fathers of the would-be brides had withheld their daughters' hands until the young men could provide more suitable dwellings.

But the trees around the woodland community were too young and none of the three young men had been able to wrestle the largest tree in the forest. Or, rather, none of them had been a match for it. They'd returned bruised both in body and in pride.

Phillip thought back to the day he'd asked Angeline's father for her hand in marriage. "If you desire her hand in marriage," the taller man had said, "then go into the forest. The time has come for you to test yourself against the trees of Angar. Provide a house, sure and strong, built from the timber of an Angar tree, and I will give you my daughter to wife."

His heart warmed as he recalled the smell of Angeline's hair as he whispered his intentions in her ear. Her blue-green eyes had shone with the splendor of emeralds as he ran his fingers through her shoulder-length auburn hair and down the smooth curve of her neck.

"I will wait for you, my Love," she'd said, kissing him on the cheek. "I will wait fifty years if necessary." Her breath passed over his ear. "But I'd prefer you not keep me waiting that long!"

Kissing her on the cheek and pulling her to himself, Phillip had left her and headed into Angar Forest. Love deep and passionate burned within his heart so that he cared for nothing else. Not for his own safety, not for his own life. There was only him and his Love.

"She is . . . beautiful," Phillip began with a sigh.

The tree rumbled thoughtfully. "What of her character?" it asked.

"She has the heart of a servant, yet she carries herself with the dignity of a princess." Phillip looked down at his bloodied hand. "And when she holds my hand the rest of the world fades as if into another universe."

Time flew by as Phillip praised Angeline. The tree did not say another word, nor did it creak again . . . though three hours passed while Phillip continued with the same line of thought that might have bored any sane man. But the tree was not a man and when the afternoon shadows lengthened it still listened.

At last Phillip let out a long sigh. "Forgive me," he said. "The time has flown by whilst I filled your mind with my heart."

The tree creaked, twisted its branches and leaned back. "Time is of no interest to one as ancient as I," it said, its leaves shivering. "But . . . your heart *is*."

Suddenly its branches bent to the ground and stretched around Phillip's legs. And though he struggled with all his might, Phillip could not free himself.

With undeniable strength the tree hauled him to within six feet of its trunk and held him there. "Do not struggle, Phillip." Two branches knifed through the air. Their leaves shrank into their stems until they looked like twin daggers aimed at his heart.

"What?! Let go of me!" Desperately Phillip fought, biting the tree's imprisoning branches with his teeth. But it did no good. Another branch encircled his neck from behind, holding it fast . . . and the twin branches stabbed into his chest. Hot tears burned in his eyes and then overflowed, running down his cheeks. As darkness swallowed him he thought he saw Angeline running toward him, screaming desperately. But darkness veiled her from sight like a cruel fog cutting him off from mortality. A mortality that he would, gladly, have lived with her.

A tremor in the earth shook the woodland community. Angeline watched, dumb-founded as a couple dozen chimneys in the row of cabins nearest her father's cracked from their bases to their tops. Bricks and mortar rained into the dirt streets connecting them.

She looked about for the cause of this disaster, at first seeing nothing. But the ground quaked again and she heard the sound of something thudding into the ground behind her. She turned to discover the cause.

Angar Forest, its many living trees rising like a protective hedge round about the community, now parted to make a very broad path. Rising from the midst of the forest, a colossal tree dwarfed all its counterparts as it sped toward her on its roots. In its branches she caught sight of her Love and with a pained scream she rushed forward.

"Angeline, no!" She could hear her father calling for her to stop, but she gave no thought to it. Somehow she had to reach Phillip.

The tree took notice of her. Its branches swiped the ground behind her, driving back her father and a couple other men. Then it entwined its branches around her torso, squeezing with the strength of iron as its roots propelled it back into the forest.

In the tree's wake Angar Forest closed off the path to any would-be-followers, the minor trees bending and weaving a natural barrier.

Angeline swooned in the tree's grasp.

Cool mist moistened his face. Phillip opened his eyes and found himself lying in direct morning sunlight. He sat up, running his hand over the soft green grass thickly decorating the meadow. A waterfall roared on its way to a clear pool of blue water a couple hundred feet from his position and a pair of pure white swans traced a graceful course over the water's surface. Various butterflies of multiple colors startled from the wildflowers growing in small patches in the meadow.

A twig snapped behind him. Jumping up and turning at the same time he held up his arms ready for battle. But instead of some foe he found Angeline lying on the ground, half-raising herself with one elbow and returning his gaze with her sparkling eyes.

"Phillip? I thought you were . . ."

He raised her to her feet, gently holding her hands and then drawing her into his embrace. "*Angeline.*" He spoke so softly that at first he thought she might not hear him. She relaxed in his arms and wrapped her arms around his body, resting her head on his chest.

As he ran his fingers through her hair and breathed a sigh of relief, a tree at the edge of the meadow caught his eye. It dwarfed the others in the thick forest surrounding the area and its bark cracked a gentle smile.

The tree creaked and its roots pulled out of the rich, brown soil. It moved toward him, towered over him. Angeline gasped and pulled out of his embrace to stand beside him. She clasped her hands to her mouth.

A branch snaked from the tree, cradling a bulbous, red thing in its crook: a human heart.

"A heart in love is a powerful thing, Phillip." The tree creaked as it held out its dagger branches, pointing them at Angeline. "Is this the woman whom you would have as your helpmate?"

Stunned to see what appeared to be *his* heart held by the tree and even more so to realize that his chest on the left side felt empty, Phillip did not at first reply. He squeezed Angeline's hand and breathed deeply to see if he was really and truly alive. "What have you done to me?" he demanded.

"Only that which I deemed necessary," the tree replied.

"Necessary?! How can you call this necessary? Am I alive? Or am I dead?"

"Oh you are not dead, Phillip." The tree's upper branches shivered in the sunlight. "You are simply crippled until I give you back your heart."

"You have no right—" Phillip began.

The tree interrupted him. "No right? Ah, but there you are wrong, young man. I have *every* right to do this." It bent its trunk toward him. The bark shifted to a frown. "I did not pick a wrestling match with you, Phillip. You *chose* to wrestle me."

"This is not wrestling."

"Isn't it though?" the tree asked. "We are in a contest. I have simply raised the stakes against you. And if you conquer me then you shall have all the wood you need to build a home for your bride . . . and not just any home, but one worthy of a great lord.

"This wrestling match could end in my death . . . but I have allowed it. Perhaps this has escaped your notice?"

Phillip clenched his fist. "I have to wrestle you for my heart?"

"No."

The tree's branch squeezed Phillip's heart and he felt as if his left breast split as the pain seared down his spine. He clutched his hollow chest and collapsed to the ground in agony.

"You have to wrestle me for your life," the tree said. "And if you by some miracle are able to overpower me then you shall have taken *my* life."

"Please." Angeline stepped toward the tree. "Please give it back. I-I won't lose him."

"So," the tree said, "you believe you are ready to be his helpmate. You will stand beside him through whatever life casts in his path? You will be loyal and honorable and lift his spirits when the going is rough?"

"That is my duty *and* my commitment; he is my Love." Angeline bit her lower lip and blood trickled from it.

"Well, my Dear." The tree squeezed Phillip's heart again, forcing him to dig his knees into the ground in order to alleviate the pain. "The going is about to get very rough."

As he gasped for breath and clutched helplessly at his hollow left breast, Phillip fought to speak. Before a single protest could leave his lips Angeline ripped her skirt to bare her smooth right leg and dashed into the midst of the tree's swiping branches. Several branches caught her face, gashing her skin. Blood pulsed from the cuts and dribbled off of her chin, but her eyes fixed on Phillip's heart. Leaping over a tree root that sought to trip her, she grabbed hold of the branch holding Phillip's heart.

This momentary distraction allowed Phillip to catch several deep, refreshing breaths. Rising to his feet and running forward, he slipped under the tree's branches and approached its trunk.

"Very well," he said, ripping off his shirt and sobering his face. "Let's wrestle."

Phillip grappled with the tree's trunk. It proved too broad for him to hold and he fell back to the ground. But he detected a smile forming in the tree's bark. He stood and dug his fingers into the tree's 'mouth' until a high-pitched creak rewarded his efforts.

Angeline screamed as the tree successfully grabbed her. Its branches coiled around her body like slippery snakes. Her eyes widened and her chest heaved to no avail. Soon the tree dropped her onto the ground . . . unmoving, still as death.

With a creaking of its thick branches, the tree squeezed Phillip's heart one more time. And as he screamed in agony over his own pain and over the sight of his gentle lover's limp body, Phillip heard the tree speak.

"Designed for man, woman was," it said. "Without her, man has only half a life . . . and his heart is hardened."

Phillip longed to scream at the villainous tree. He longed to rip its limbs from its trunk with his bare hands. What could have caused it to extinguish a life as pure, as innocent, as selfless, and as brave as Angeline's? She had not deserved this. She deserved to live a full life and a long one, full of children and joy.

"If—I—could," he spat at the tree in spite of its cruel grasp on his heart. "If I could be free then would I kill you, Tree. But now I am left with nothing. My life is over. Kill me now or I will do so myself."

Suddenly the tree's bark cracked into a smile broad enough for three men to stand in and it chuckled in a voice so deep, so old, that the ground trembled beneath Phillip's feet. It pricked Angeline's arm with a branch and her chest heaved a breath. "Now *that*, Phillip, is the sort of love I am willing to die for!"

CAPTAIN KANOVI: THE FATE OF THE CAPTAIN AND HIS FIRST MATE

The Captain looked his First Mate in the eye.
"We can't leave port!" was his cry.
"No sir, not now with the wind to stern,
And it's too bad. On this cargo we'd have had return."

With nothing but sails on their vessel
Only a good wind could serve to propel
Them and their rich cargo
To their destination before the morrow.

So the two men paced from prow to stern
And with all their beings did they yearn
For the wind to change in their favor
And make their futures that much brighter.

If a fortune was to be made from their cargo
Then tonight they should leave; not tomorrow.
But the clouds looked none too friendly
And a storm was coming surely

The breeze was still adverse and thunder rumbled
Then as the poor captain grumbled
Lightning zipped across the sky
And he clenched his fists as time flew by.

A little fishy creature flipped over the rise.
But they knew not what to do in their surprise.
They simply watched as it flipped and played
(For the creature was a beautiful mermaid!)

"Why have happiness you denied?
For the sea is peppered with the tears you cried."
She said this to ease their troubled minds but to her chagrin,
What should happen? But they both dove in!

The water was rough and the waves high
And though she searched not a trace of them she spied.
So the legend goes that Captain Kanovi,
With his first mate, left life early.

They died together because of a mermaid's cry
Intended to aid them by and by.
But such was the fate
Of the captain and his mate!

SPLINTERED SACRIFICE

With a sigh that sounded as hollow as a night wind, and a creak as old as the earth itself, the oak tree drooped its branches. All around it, where once had been a million other boughs as strong as its own, a billion other leaves as vibrantly green, a thousand trunks thick and hard, there was now a flat wasteland.

A young woman stood near at branch, a string-fitted longbow held in one hand and a short sword in her other. Her hair was red as a rose's petals, and the unrelenting breath of cold wind coming from the east froze her cheeks into a paler hue of the same color.

The tree's branches drooped despite the rays of sunlight spilling from the eastern horizon.

In the distance, from the north, the tree felt the encroaching hoards of another tyrant bent on crossing the wasteland, determined to pass over the corpses of those who'd fallen before on the quest for greater power, more dominion. The hoards of men with spear and ax, melded to the would-be-conqueror's will. The clang of their weapons was offensive to the tree. They had no respect to nature, no desire to better themselves beyond what they were. They would not stop to consider, to listen, to patiently learn before stepping out into a world they knew little about.

If, the tree reasoned, the Creator had wanted men to be this way, then he would have sent them clear instructions to do so. And he would not have bothered with the crafting of trees and all manner of animals and insects. Instead he would have made a dull world, colorless, without a sunrise such as the one now occurring.

To the south was all that remained of a people worthy of creation, who knew not war but cared for the gardens in which the Creator had placed them. And around the gardens (which were far to the south, beyond sight over the horizon) there had once been a vast ring of trees like this one.

The tree sighed again, recalling how his brethren and sister trees had, one by one, fulfilled their purpose. His day would come, the tree had known. He just wished he had a little more time.

"They come," the rose-haired woman said simply. Without even glancing over her shoulder at the tree she held her hand toward its branches. "Are you ready?"

It took the tree a long while to reply. Stretching out its branches it saw the enemy come on the run, yelling at the top of their lungs.

Suddenly, with a painful twist that felt like ripping its heart out, the tree broke one of its branches and laid it on the ground by the woman. The sap bled from the rip, and the tree hardened its bark before ripping another branch from its trunk.

As each branch was laid beside her, the woman cut them into angry shafts which she notched to her bowstring and sent into the oncoming warriors. Fast and accurate she shot the arrows, using up the branches as quickly as the tree could sacrifice them.

At the end, when the hoards of men had been reduced to a small mob, she cut into the naked tree's trunk. The last of its sap flowed, the last of its fragments lodged in the assailants' hearts.

In the end nothing of the tree remained, save for a bit of root dying in the sunlight. But a few shoots split the earth, coming forth to grow, and the woman waited. Another day might come when the trees could again serve their purpose.

THE WOODLAND KING

Stepping along the white stone path to the twisted wood throne of the Woodland King, Lyric kept her eyes lowered in respect. "You called for me, my Lord?"

The king did not at first reply. He rose from his throne, his long shadow falling over her, and she heard the sound of feathered wings passing over her head and fluttering onto his shoulder as his phoenix landed. "Lyric, how long have you been with me?" The king's voice was gentle, every word marked with the affection he held her in.

She baited her breath, thinking back to the day she had wandered into his forest. "It has been three years," she replied.

"One thousand and ninety-five days . . . . In all that time you have been patient with me and have expected that I will fulfill my end of our bargain." He stepped toward her and raised her chin with his wrinkled hand.

She looked into his face. The faded green eyes had not lost their energy, and his silvery hair only added to the trust she felt for him.

"My dear child," the king said, "you came to me when you were only sixteen years old, though it seems like a lifetime has passed." He sighed and kissed her forehead. "So beautiful you were, and you are beautiful still.

"I promised you that I would give you a song from the King of Heaven and now the time has come for me to give it to you. I caution you: you are not the first to come. I gave this song to others, many others. All of them sang the song, all of them saw the paths and every last one of them chose the wrong one."

Lyric felt a shiver of excitement mingled with uncertainty run up her spine. Three years ago, in this very woods—she could remember every awful detail as if it were yesterday—she had been sitting on a green moss-covered log.

Rupert had been there too, sitting beside her. He had been her childhood playmate, a peasant lad assigned by her father to look out for her. He had said something unthinkable to her.

"I know your father thinks of me as nothing more than a servant, Lyric, but you have treated me as your equal." He'd reached out and held her hand while looking into her eyes and spoken of love and told her how he felt about her.

Perhaps it had been the way she'd been brought up to believe that a peasant should never approach a noble-born. Perhaps she'd been afraid of ruining their friendship by admitting that she felt that way about him. Whatever the reason—if there was one—Lyric had playfully pushed him away, sending him rolling down a forest slope into the dark swamp. She had searched for him, long and hard, regretting her deed. Then, when she'd given up all hope for him, the old man known as the woodland king had found her weeping.

"You promised, my lord, to give me a song when I had served you for three years. You promised me a song that would undo my wrong."

"And so I did," he murmured, gently lifting the bright gold phoenix from his shoulder and setting it on hers. "The song of the King of

Heaven will come to you, as it did to those before you. Let the phoenix guide your song. If your motives prove pure then your heart will truly be healed. Many have failed to do this. Do you wish to proceed?"

"What if I fail?"

"To sing the song?"

She nodded slowly and he smiled encouragement.

"You can sing the song, Lyric. All that remains to be seen is if you will sing the song of the King of Heaven and then choose the right path, or the path that is most convenient."

The song of the King of Heaven. Those words washed over her like a warm flood. Closing her eyes, she felt herself rise into the air, and when she opened her eyes she was standing above the clouds.

Spreading its wings, the phoenix warbled a series of deep, musical notes that sounded like they'd been strummed from a harp. Its black eyes glanced down its hooked beak at Lyric as it continued its song. The notes reverberated against the clouds, holding their volume, and the bird fed more notes into the air until they streamed together into a beautiful blend, yet she could tell that it was somehow incomplete.

The phoenix looked down at her again, this time it squawked and nuzzled her.

"But I don't know what to sing," Lyric protested. As the words left her mouth, they joined the music already created by the phoenix.

In a heartbeat the fluffy moisture billowing around her transformed. She found herself standing in a field of green grass that stretched to the horizon. The sun was directly overhead, bright but not hot. Not even a breeze stirred the grass.

"Hello, Lyric."

She turned and fell immediately to her knees. Before her stood a smiling man robed in pure white. His face shone with holy light and in his outstretched hands he held a gold book.

"Do you fear me, Lyric?"

She shook her head, even though she felt shaken, but he took her hand and pulled her up by the arm.

"Rise, child, I am but a messenger bearing the glory of the One who sent me. Do not pay homage to me. There is only One, the King of Heaven, who deserves to be treated in this way."

Trembling, she stood as he released his hold on her arm. "Where am I?" It was the first thing that came to her lips.

"You are at the Crossroads. Here you will choose which path suits you."

"Do not listen to that false prophet!" Another man, shining with blinding brilliance, had appeared to her left. Only he had—wings! An angel? Or, were they both? "Lyric," the blindingly bright angel cried, "you have sung the song of the King of Heaven and now you must make a choice. The right choice."

The first angel stepped closer to her and laid his hand on her shoulder. "Many have come here before, Lyric, and all of them have listened to the Master of Lies. You too may listen, but only at the same terrible cost that he exacts." He pulled her around and gazed into her eyes. The phoenix flapped its wings for balance.

"But how do I know—" she hesitated, "how do I know which of you is the Father of Lies?"

The angel's smile broadened. "The choices you are offered will open your eyes . . . . Observe!" He pointed behind her. She turned around.

Two roads now cut through the endless field, one to the right and one to the left. To her right the road was wide and smooth. At its end—standing waiting for her—was Rupert! She almost ran immediately to him, thinking her sorrow at an end, but she noticed the road that led to the left. It was narrow and crooked. At its end was another Rupert, this one looking weary and bloodied on the forehead by some blade.

"But—what? I don't—"

"What? You don't understand?" the winged angel asked. "It's really very simple, Lyric: go down the easy path and avoid any injury to yourself or your lover, or follow the narrow way and end up on your death bed with only a moment to say goodbye to the lad. I know it sounds easy, almost too good to be true, but it is true."

She turned to the first angel. "Will both roads lead me to Rupert?"

"No, Lyric, they will not. One leads to a fantasy, the other leads to your death and Rupert's life."

"My death?" She stumbled back from him, accidentally knocking into the winged angel.

"Fantasy or not, the right path is your way," the second angel said. "Follow it and I promise you happiness for eternity!"

"No." She pushed him away and stroked the phoenix's breast with her fingers as it crooned. "It is you. You are the Father of Lies!"

"Come now," the angel cackled. "How did you come to that conclusion?"

She stepped onto the left-hand path, cringing as its hot stones singed her bare feet. "The King of Heaven would not bargain," she said under her breath. "You tell me to follow your path, but no! I will not. Rupert must live, what happens to me—no longer matters."

Before the angel could say another word and before she could reconsider her choice, she raced down the crooked path. Stones overturned, tripping her and each of them burned her skin as it made contact.

The phoenix flew from her shoulder and circled overhead, singing encouragement. The closer she came to the end—the nearer she came to reaching Rupert—the more painful the path became. When her feet had blistered raw, and her body had been bruised from falling on the stones, Lyric could continue no farther. She fell one last time.

Light gave way to darkness and she lost consciousness.

"Lyric," Rupert's voice whispered in her ear as if from a great distance.

She opened her eyes, afraid of what she might see. The Woodland King's great golden phoenix stood beside her head, silent. It cocked its head to the side, its intelligent black eyes scanning her face. Her head throbbed and she reached for it with her left hand, but someone else's was holding it and a gentle hand stroked her dark hair out of her eyes.

What, or who? Lyric tried to sit up and struggled to see through the weariness that suddenly came over her. Am I dead?

"Lyric . . . wake up," the voice said, this time closer.

At last her vision cleared and she looked about, startling herself with a girlish scream. "Rupert!" He looked not a day older than she remembered, yet his eyes were greener than she recalled and his face sincere, as if he had gained wisdom beyond his years. "Is it really you?" she managed.

"Yes, Lyric. It is really I."

"But how? I thought you were dead . . . . You fell—"

He shook his head slightly, gazing into her eyes with an affection that made her forget all else. "I could never leave you, Lyric, and I was afraid that you did not truly love me." He stood to his feet and she caught her breath as he transfigured into the man that she knew as the Woodland King.

"It was you? You wanted me to sing the song of the King of Heaven? Why?"

Returning into the familiar youthful form of her lover, Rupert knelt by her side and took her hand. "Because only by singing the song and passing the test could you prove that your love was true, and now I know that it is and we will never again be parted. For I have given my heart to you and you have given your life for mine."

THE PRIZE OF SACRIFICE

"Men of wickedness are in abundance, and they disguise themselves from my eyes in many different ways," proclaimed the king to his subjects. "I have no son, only a daughter. You know her, my people. She is upright and lovely to behold. It is well known that the man who wins her hand from me will inherit the kingdom and it is known to me that many unworthy men have tried to gain her hand in marriage.

"Therefore, I have arranged for my friend the dragon to hold my precious daughter in the heart of Mount Purity. A series of tests have been arranged for each and every man that dares to enter the gates on the mountain's southern slope. These tests will sift the wicked-hearted from him that is worthy. To the man that passes the tests, will be awarded the prize: my only daughter."

The king, standing upon a large balcony of his castle, drew a sword and raised it to the sky. "Hail the mighty one, my trusted friend, Valorian!"

A four-legged dragon as dark as night with yellow eyes shot through the overhanging clouds, angled his veined wings back, and settled next to the king. With one clawed hand he received the sword that the king held.

"Bring me the princess!" Valorian hissed. The ladies in the crowd fainted as the dark-haired princess emerged from the castle onto the balcony and the dragon grabbed her.

Princes from neighboring lands were in the crowd. They drew their swords, shouted insults at the dragon, and then ran toward the southern slope of Mount Purity. The dragon leapt into the wind, beat his powerful wings, and zipped out of the crowd's sight in the direction of Mount Purity.

Having seen all this, Morgrin, who was a faithful knight, despaired for the princess's life. He had served in the king's presence for many years and he had grown fond of the king's daughter. He was not a prince and, though he knew that the proclamation had been intended as an invitation to men of royal blood, he determined that he would do all in his power to rescue the girl and bring her out of the dragon's clutches.

The king might trust Valorian, but that seemed foolish to Morgrin. *Doesn't the king love his daughter?* He thought. *If so, why put her through this pain? Is it possible that the king is merely bored and this is for his entertainment?*

Rage filled him and he squared his shoulders. Prince or not, he would go to his lady's aid. Checking to ensure that his trusted scimitar was sheathed at his side, he filled his canteen at the village fountain, and set out in pursuit of the princes.

The overcast skies flashed with lightning as he neared the mountain. Rain splattered against the ground, wetting the earth around his feet. He quickened his pace and headed for the wrought iron gates set into the mountainside. One lone prince remained outside the gates, trembling in his shoes.

"Greetings, my Prince!" Morgrin hailed him as he stepped out of the rain and into the shelter of the overhanging rocks. "Looks like a storm is brewing."

The prince laughed nervously and wiped his sweaty forehead. "To which storm do you refer? That which awaits those entering Mount Purity, or that which is building in the skies?"

"Both I guess." He paused to survey the young man. "Are you ill, Sir?"

He did not answer. Instead he cleared his throat, marched up to the gates, and tried the latch. It did not budge and he furrowed his brow. "How very strang.... The other princes opened these with ease."

Morgrin stepped up beside him, lifted the latch, and the gates swung inward. A funnel of air sucked him inside and he held on tightly to his sheathed sword. *If I lose this, I will be a dead man!* When the air stilled he found that he was standing inside the mountain and the prince was still trapped outside the gates.

Shrugging his shoulders to ward off the chill, he proceeded into the passageway. Torches lined the walls of stone, casting flickering light over the path. He could hear the sounds of battle ahead and he saw fire shoot through the darkness. Running, he came onto a broad plane of rock. Six princes, with shields raised and swords drawn, were fighting for their lives against Valorian. But the dragon's dark scales made it easy for him to flit unseen through the darkness and attack them when it was to his advantage.

First one prince fell, burned from behind his back. Then another was plucked off the ground and hurled against the wall, falling limp to the stone floor. Valorian disappeared again only to reemerge moments later spewing flames and striking with his sharp claws until the remaining princes were defeated.

Morgrin felt the dragon's yellow eyes bore into him. The creature stepped over its victims, growled, and then sprang at him. Morgrin rolled on the ground, under the dragon's belly, and pitched sideways just as Valorian smashed down his tail. Suddenly, the dragon stopped his attack and its yellow eyes grew big.

"Morgrin?" he asked. "Morgrin the knight?"

Bowing to the creature, Morgrin sheathed his sword. "Yes, it is I."

The dragon scratched his head. "What are you doing here?"

"Just seeing to it that none of these fools becomes king, my lord."

"But you are a knight. Even if you win this contest the king is not likely to give you his daughter, or his throne."

"That was not my intention, my lord Valorian. I only care to ensure that none of these princes win the king's daughter."

Valorian shook his head. "I cannot permit you to pass into the heart of this mountain. The king charged me with proving a worthy heir to the throne." He pointed a claw at the passage that led out of the mountain. "Return, Morgrin, for you are an honorable knight and I do not wish to kill you."

"So, you will not let me pass?"

"Sorry, my brave knight. It would be against the rules."

Morgrin placed a hand on his hip and pointed his other in the creature's face. "Two years ago a young man saved a dragon from certain death. Do you remember?" He drew his sword and ran his finger along the flat of the blade. "The dragon slayers had hauled their prey from the skies and one of them raised this scimitar to kill the dragon, but a young man of humble beginnings came and saved the dragon from the slayers. Do you remember that day?"

"Aye, Morgrin. I remember it all too well, for it was *you* that rescued me and your deed placed you in high standing with the king." Valorian struck the stone floor. "But I am honor bound and I cannot allow you to pass!"

"I am not requesting you to *allow* my passage, Valorian. All I ask is that you give me the same opportunity as those fools you roasted."

A smile creased the dragon's face. "Very well, Morgrin. I will give you a fair trial. But be forewarned: I will not soften my blows and you may fall beside these 'fools.'"

"I would not expect you to!" Morgrin raced to the slain princes and hefted one of their shields in his hand. "One more thing, Valorian?"

"Yes?"

"How many champions have passed on to the next test?"

"Twenty-four," the dragon replied. He pulled back his neck, breathed in air, and heaved a long, and tortuous blaze in Morgrin's direction.

As tongues of fire raged past his shield, sweat broke out on Morgrin's face and ran off his chin. The fiery assault continued without abating. He could feel the heat building up around him, as if he were a turkey roasting in a brick oven. Valorian was renowned for his ability to breath a seemingly endless stream of flames. If Morgrin remained here he would soon fall. He looked about and found the body of a fallen prince nearby. Propping the body against his shield, he grabbed another shield and backed away from the dragon toward the opposite end of the battlefield.

While the dragon roasted the already dead prince, he searched until he found the exit tunnel in the back of the cavern. It was too small for Valorian to follow. He hunkered down and waited until the dragon ceased his assault on the corpse.

Valorian walked toward the shield and from where he was hiding Morgrin saw the shield collapse and the body fall. The dragon made a little cry and then called to the corpse. "Morgrin?" Valorian stood over the prince's body and the shield and he started to cry. "Oh, Morgrin, my friend! My brave friend . . . . I am so sorry."

At first, Morgrin thought of revealing himself to the dragon. But he stopped himself. *If I don't make it through the other tests, then Valorian would grieve twice.* He sighed. *It is better if he thinks I am dead.*

Morgrin trudged through ankle-deep mud in the tunnel and when he reached its end he was relieved to find an open, dry arena. A brawny man of great height stood at the arena's center wielding a long sword. "Welcome to your next test, Gent!" the man bellowed. "I am the Sword Master and if you cannot best me then you will end up like this man." He picked a groaning prince off the floor, set him in a slide, and released him. The prince slid down the slide and out of sight through the rock wall. "Fall in or be counted out!"

"Hello, Rock!" Morgrin greeted him as he stepped into the dim torchlight. "How'd you get involved in this fiasco?"

"Morgrin? My word, it is you! What are you doing here? You aren't a prince."

Morgrin chuckled and moved closer. "No. No. I am not a prince."

"Then what are you doing here?" The man held up his hand. "Wait! Don't tell me . . .." He narrowed his eyes. "The princess?"

Morgrin made no reply.

"My friend," Rock said, "I told you long ago that she's out of your class. You should look for a gal within your means."

"Are you saying that I am not worthy?"

"No, of course not! I've enjoyed trouncing these princes because I know that they are not like you." He breathed deeply. "I know that you love her, Morgrin. But you must let go."

"I will pass, my friend," Morgrin replied, "whether you stand in my way or not." He balanced his scimitar in his hand and took another step.

The Sword Master grinned broadly. "Come now, Morgrin! You know that I am the stronger man. You don't have a chance of getting past me!"

Morgrin nodded then clacked his tongue. "Your wife would fully sympathize with me—though I would hope it wouldn't be necessary to tell her about this." He shook his head. "She would not approve of your opposing me."

Rock swallowed and bit his lip. "Ah, you wouldn't do that to me—would you?"

"Well, let's see now." Morgrin scratched his chin. "If you were in my place and the princess was your wife, then what would *you* do?"

A light dawned in the larger man's eyes. He stepped aside and waved toward a door behind him. "Go after her, my friend! I will not be the one to stop you."

Shaking the man's hand and thanking him, Morgrin opened the door and passed through. "I won't forget this, Rock."

"Greetings, young master," a female voice said to him. He looked around in wonder. A field of green grass now surrounded him and he was standing in the shade of a yellow-leafed tree. A young woman clad in a white dress was extending her hand to him.

"Greetings," he said. "Where am I?"

She kept her eyes lowered and spoke softly. "I am your guide for the remainder of your journey. Come!" She took his hand and led him to the far side of the field.

From the ground arose a large, glass building. A sign over its entrance doors read: Warrior's Enclave. She brought him inside, gave him money, and showed him around the store. Swords of exquisite and wonderful designs lined the walls. There were shields too, as well as daggers, bows, and darts. A wide selection of armor was available as well. Having only the money that she had given him, Morgrin selected a new sword and proceeded to the counter.

As he was laying the money on the table he noticed a little boy kneeling by the counter. A little cup was in his grimy hands and rags adorned his frail body. *What is a beggar doing here?* He cancelled his purchase, knelt beside the beggar, and filled his cup with money.

"God bless you, Sir!" said the lad, grinning from ear to ear.

Morgrin smiled back, tussled the little fellow's hair, and walked out of the store. As soon a he stepped outside the building, it, the young woman, and the field disappeared. Now, instead of standing on beautiful green grass, he was walking down a cobble-stoned street. Deserted, empty houses lined the way and the revolting smell of rotting flesh drove his senses crazy.

Turning a corner, he was startled to see the young woman from the field walking toward him. This time her eyes were bold and her dress revealed her appealing form. The wind toyed with her long, wavy hair. As she came near, she kissed him on the cheek, and laughed. "You are a true gentleman, Morgrin—giving your money to the beggar and leaving the beautiful sword!" She pulled on his arm. "Come, I must show you something!"

They neared a house on the right hand side of the street. Its windows were new, its paint was fresh, and bright curtains adorned the windows. She pulled him toward the door, but suddenly he froze. She turned. "Come! What are you doing?"

"'For the lips of a strange woman drop as an honeycomb, and her mouth is smoother than oil: But her end is bitter as wormwood, sharp as a two edged sword.'" The words had come to him from memory and from Scripture. He shoved her away, ignoring her hurt look and distressed exclamation. He walked down the street until it wilted around him, like a forest of flowers dying from lack of water.

In place of the harlot's dead town he was now surrounded by another stone tunnel. This time, however, the tunnel ahead of him ended abruptly. A great chasm lay before him and on the opposite side he saw Valorian, his black head lowered as if in conversation with the princess on the ledge. There was a narrow, wooden bridge spanning the abyss.

"It seems that I was right, Princess," the dragon rumbled. "It is as I feared: no man worthy of your hand has come."

"If only Father had not insisted on a man of royal birth." She hung her head in her hands. "There was one man that I would give my heart to in a moment, but he was not among them."

Morgrin stepped onto the bridge. His legs felt weary from the day's toil and his hands trembled. Realizing that he had come to the final test, he allowed himself a moment of rest. But the bridge snapped under his weight and he realized, too late, that it was a trap.

The princess screamed and heard her plead with Valorian. The dragon swooped upon him, grasped him in his talons, and set him safely on the ledge. "Now," Valorian said, raising a claw, "you have saved my life and I have saved yours: we are even."

Panting for breath, Morgrin looked into the eyes of the princess. They were honest, pure, and intelligent. She looked lovely. He reached out to take her hand and she reached for his. "No!" The dragon slammed himself between them. "You have not passed the final test."

Drawing back his hand, Morgrin glared. "Now what?"

Valorian drew out the sword that the king had given him from a sheath under his wing and a great tear rolled from his eye. "My friend, I am so sorry. I thought I saw you die once, yet somehow you lived, and now—when you have survived—there remains the hardest one of all." He glanced at the princess. "It was by her father's decree that this be done." He set the sword on the ledge, grabbed the princess, and vaulted into the air, circling slowly. "Three tests you have passed, yet the last is most difficult."

"Tell me, Valorian!" Morgrin screamed. "Tell me, now!"

"I am under orders, my friend: if the winner does not slay himself on this sword then the girl must be dropped into the abyss! I am sorry—very sorry. And it shames me that this is the king's will, but I must obey."

Morgrin picked up the sword and shook it at the dragon. "Let me see if I understand you correctly: commit suicide and she lives, don't do it and you throw her into the pit?"

Only a nod was the creature's reply.

"You know that I love her, Valorian, and I know that you will keep your word, thus—" he held the sword's point over his heart and balanced the pommel between two stones. "Promise me one thing, my friend?"

The dragon choked on his words. "Anything."

"Do not give her back into the king's hand, for he is undeserving of selecting her husband." Again the dragon nodded. Morgrin, before he could think twice, fell on the sword and darkness filled his vision. He could feel warm, sticky blood pooling around his hands—it was his blood. He felt the ledge shake as the dragon landed and heard the voice of his lover as she called for him to rise. But he could not muster the strength and soon he lost all sense—of anything—anything except, that is, for a voice inside his mind.

"Wake up, son of honor, your worth you have proved! I am the sword that divides the true from the false, the righteous from the liar, and the wise from the fool. You have earned that which you love, for she is the prize of your sacrifice!"

Morgrin rose a new man, strengthened, renewed. His sight was restored and he saw his love kneeling before him with tears raining from her eyes. He lifted her face and smiled when he saw her astonishment.

Valorian, great dragon as he was, was so astounded that he almost fainted. "My friend, you live!"

"Yes, Valorian, I do live. And so does she. In the wake of sacrifice is the reward and, this time, the reward of sacrifice is the woman I love."

"But what of the king? What will he think?"

"The king need not know, my friend." Morgrin took the sword

on which he had impaled himself and slid it into his scabbard. Looking into the dragon's face, he pointed upward. "Just set me and my bride in the distant forest."

Valorian grinned, showing all his teeth, allowed Morgrin and the girl to mount, and then he launched into the air above the abyss. "It will be as you say, Morgrin. The king will not know."

THE WORLD REBORN

The blind and barren wastes call their children home. Leafless trees in eternal evening beneath clouded skies, beckon with their branches across the desert. The wind whips across the sands and gives the trees voices . . . and they call, "Return, Edmond, return. Come back to Avaron, thy beloved and forsaken kingdom. Return with life, wife, and child. Restore the water, channel it into the sands. Take spade and pickax with you. Dig into the sand, pull it away from our roots. For its salt doth eat our life. Fill us with water and surround our roots with soil. Then would we raise you on a throne of hickory and gird you with ash."

Into the distance the wind carries their voices. Over the sand it passes, into the horizon. The wind stretches over a dry grassy plain, and the land dips into a vast valley. There, surrounded by dead and dying flora, lies a lake bed. A small pond sparkles in its midst, the last remnant of that once generous supply of water.

The wind strikes it and the trees' voices splash like pebbles on the pond's surface. The water springs up, the wind twists it and an enormous bubble is formed. It floats skyward and enters the atmosphere, then sails into the stars.

Edmond's space bubble spun around him. He twisted his arm in the organic blue cables that held him fast. The cables stretched him out as if crucifying him, and his bubble elongated into the stars. Space warped around him. The various stars in their varied colors, streamed past, and moments later the bubble reformed into a perfect sphere and the cords relaxed. He smiled at the blue sun rising over the darkened planetoid ahead of him.

Turning, he pressed his lips to the soapy inner surface of the space bubble. "I've come home, darling . . . Everything is prepared. Please join me when you are able." The soap stuck to his lips as he pulled back and blew into it, forming a small bubble that billowed into space and broke away from his space bubble.

Floating through black space, the bubble elongated, humming with a voice of its own. Energy sparked along its shiny surface, speeding it away from him. It shot into the stars, vanishing from sight.

He faced the blue sun and grunted as he flexed his arms, drawing taut the cords. The space bubble gurgled and glided toward the planet. The dark planet rose to meet him and the sun formed a blue halo around it. Touching the atmosphere, the bubble bounced a few times before making a gradual descent through it.

Far below lay the desert wastes that once he called home. He stretched his arms over his head and the cords released him. He closed his eyes, curling into a fetal position. The bubble suspended him in its midst and lukewarm air lulled him to sleep.

As she sat on the tower's pinnacle platform, Sara gazed heavenward. Her husband had tried many times to reach his long-lost home. That dying planetoid called to him. Ever since the message bubble had arrived with that haunting plea, Edmond had searched.

She sighed and kissed her infant daughter's forehead. The child crooned and shook her rattle with a toothless smile.

Suddenly the dark sky brightened and a bubble glided toward her. She stood as it approached and, as it hovered before her, she popped it with a finger.

"I've come home, darling . . . Everything is prepared. Please join me when you are able," the bubble said with its dying breath.

Twirling in a little dance, she held her infant high and then laughed. She ran off the roof and plummeted into the corn fields. But a space bubble rose from the ground. She bounced inside it and pulled at the organic cords draped along its interior surface. The bubble rose high into the air and all around her larger space bubbles rose from the corn fields. Some were filled with seeds, some held water.

The bubble fleet left the planet. They rolled into space and stretched in preparation for instant inter star transport. Space rippled around her and warped.

The space bubble sent a waking jolt down Edmond's arm. He stood and grabbed the organic cords. Less than a mile below him stretched the desert, its large trees mere skeletons of their former selves. His bubbled plummeted the remaining distance and popped on a tree's branch.

He fell to the hard ground, still holding the organic cords in his hands. The broken bubble had splashed onto the tree's cracked branches. What little liquid there was, soaked into the bark. The tree creaked, its branches trembled, and it leaned toward him. He lashed the organic cords around its trunk and stood back. The cords melded with the tree and its roots stretched beneath his feet.

"Not yet, old friend," he said, glancing at the night sky. "But this world may begin a new rotation . . . for here it comes."

The sky lightened and the stars vanished. Space bubbles burst into view. A host of them rained upon the planet. As each of them popped their contents spilled. They watered the ground and seeded it. The trees lurched out of the hard earth, dancing around him as leaves budded on their branches. Bubbles continued to fall. Streams flowed to the horizon and grass grew.

A distance away a smaller space bubble fell. It rolled toward him along the land. It stopped nearby and his wife carried their child out of it. The bubble trembled as she left it, but it held together. He ran to her and they embraced. The trees danced around them, speared their roots deep in the ground, entwined their branches, and grew high over his head. A veritable pyramid of wood formed and the roots laced over the ground to create a floor. At one end the trees left an arched exit.

He led his wife by the arm and they stepped into the brightening landscape. Before them a tree grew a hundred feet broad and rose to an incalculable height. Wind swept the land, giving the tree a voice. "Your kingdom awakens, Edmond. Avaron bows and sings thanks to God."

Edmond bowed and stepped forward. "Let this land be renewed. Let the waters run again and the crops will grow." Then he raised his fist and opened it toward the great tree. "Shall this world be renewed? Will the sun rise in the day and set at evening? Or will we live in darkness?"

The wind rushed through the tree, "It shall!" And the enormous branches reached down to the earth and divided it.

Edmond stepped back and knelt at the edge of the division.

The tree's branches burrowed to a vast depth until he could see the planet's molten core. The branches wrapped around the core and the enormous tree leapt into the hole. It fell to the planet's core, roots and branches moving in swift, pulling motions until the core began to turn.

The hole in the earth sealed itself shut and the ground lurched. His wife cried out and as she stumbled he caught her.

But as he smiled into her face the blue sun rose over the horizon and flowers grew. Where the land had been blind and barren, light and life returned.

ROSWELL'S COUSIN

Swatting away the noxious vapors drifting from the gaping barrel of his revolver, Harlan shook his head, disgust turning to relief as his gaze fastened on the dead man lying in the dust. Another criminal wiped off the map, one less bounty hunter to deal with.

Harlan swiveled on his heel—and froze.

The ranch house, his house, it stood to his right, and to the left and beyond stretched flat Texas land. And perched amidst his scattering herds of long horned cattle, the harsh solar heat radiated off of a silvery disc. Not small, not big. Perhaps the breadth of his shed. Most definitely not as high, but squashed flat, with a single orb protrusion in its center.

Three bounty hunters in the past several days, now dead, and now this *thing* suddenly appearing in the back yard; perhaps this new hiding place had not been such a great choice after all.

He adjusted his twelve-gallon hat higher on his head, not that it or his cowboy getup could disguise his New York accent and unblemished face. But it felt right to look his best. Who knew? Mayhap one of these days Victor Bell's cronies would land a lucky shot, and Harlan would exist—no more.

Picking his slow route over the dry grass and through the occasional clouds of dust, he made his way within ten feet of the silvery disc.

Oddly enough, the strange thing reminded him of that story someone he knew believed. It had something to do with a spaceship crashing into Earth, and a big government cover-up. Roswell? Yes, Roswell, and the media had latched onto some guy's story about aliens being aboard the craft while the government claimed it had been a weather balloon.

Harlan had never been swayed one way or the other. All that mattered for the moment? The answer to that was easy: getting away from the thugs who wanted his money, getting away to live, not just exist on the run.

Hissing air drew his attention back to the disc. The middle orb-thing popped open and a tall, thin figure in a green suit stepped up and out. And Harlan found himself looking up at a glass-dome helmet and the biggest pair of white eyes imaginable. No pupils, just big, round white eyes set in a face as green as New York grass, and a tiny round mouth kissing at him.

Later, Harlan swore by his life that he did not pass out, but he, curiously, had no memory of what transpired immediately following the alien's appearance.

"Earthling," the tall being's voice resonated inside its helmet as it stepped daintily toward Harlan on its toothpick legs. It blinked its big eyes.

Harlan felt dizzy but he forced himself to stand. He found himself looking, dumbfounded, at the green being. "Yes?" he said, feeling stupid.

"Earthling, I come find Roswell. Where Roswell?"

"Roswell?!" He shrugged and then laughed. "How should I know? They took the stuff to Area 51 according to the papers."

The alien stretched out a long, spindly arm. Three thin fingers clamped over his shoulder and hauled him onto the silvery disc of the spaceship.

"Hey! Take it easy, Pal!" He held his revolver's barrel to the alien's bubble helmet. The transparent material bent inward but bounced back just as quickly; so much for it being made of glass.

"Earthling, you come with me."

"Where?" The alien's green face scrunched up and Harlan lifted his eyebrows. "Not Area 51? Look, Pal, I was kidding. It doesn't even exist." Doubt filled his mind as he glanced over the being's outfit, all green. "You're for real, aren't you? I mean, you're not from my neck of the woods, are you?"

Tilting its head sideways, the alien's white eyes seemed to assess him.

"Roswell, must find Roswell."

Harlan held up his hand, still training his revolver on the alien's face. "I think you're confused, Pal. Roswell is a place. I meant that the papers postulated that our government," he ran his fingers through the air, "*moved* the items *to* Area 51."

"Then I must go, Earthling." The alien stepped into the cockpit, arms and legs folded, taking up very little space as it started pressing multi-colored buttons. "Thank you for help."

A motor roared in the distance. Harlan turned, looked past the ranch house to the road. A Bronco, racing full speed, approached, two men leaned out the open back windows hefting—sniper rifles!

As the first shot sounded, missing wildly but shattering a window in the ranch house, Harlan knocked on the now-closing alien cockpit.

"Yes, Earthling?" The spaceship's top rose by increments. "Is there something else?" The alien's white eyes waited patiently.

"Yes," another gun fired, the bullet ricocheted off the space disc. "Yes, yes, yes!" Harlan said, "You need to bring me with you."

The alien did not move a muscle. "Explain."

"The government is bad," Harlan rushed, trying to ignore the sound of more guns going off. "Very bad government. You need me to get inside."

At this the alien's eyes shrank to half their size. "You are mistaken, Earthling."

"No I'm not! The security is very tight—yes—very tight at Area 51. But they are always looking for more of you guys to perform their experiments on! So you need me to pretend to bring you in for them to study, otherwise you'll never step one foot near *Roswell.*" He emphasized the final word, hoping his ploy would buy him his chance.

Without a word, the alien reached up and yanked him inside the small cockpit. Another bullet ricocheted off the silver spaceship as the eight-foot-tall alien punched multi-colored buttons and the ship levitated, then moved, soundless, into the clouds.

"Yeah, I'm a civilian," Harlan yelled into the guards' ears. "What of it? If you had one of these," he shook his revolver at the alien standing, head hanging, white eyes wide open, "turn up in your mother's back yard, would you stop her from coming in? Don't think I won't take this to the papers! The country will be in a fine mess if you don't' open those doors."

The sergeant got on the phone and, moments later, opened the bunker door. "Elevator shaft'll take you to the forty-seventh level down. They'll be waiting for you. And—Sir—your firearm?"

Harlan shook his head and made a disapproving grunt in his throat. "Land of the free, home of the brave; what happened to all that?"

He stepped into the elevator with his alien "captive" and two guards. As soon as the elevator began its descent, he clobbered the guy next to him, knocking him out. The other guard, gawking at the tall alien, dropped his gun and put his hands on his head.

The alien touched the man's arm and, withdrawing his fingers, left a needle in his skin. The guard's eyes closed, his mouth eased into a smile and he collapsed to the elevator floor.

"Now what?"

"Where would they keep Roswell?" the alien asked.

"Highest security area will likely be on the lowest level," Harlan scratched his chin. "That ship is real important to you, isn't it?"

"Ship?" The alien swept the air with both thin arms, reminding Harlan of an octopus under water. "Not a ship . . . Roswell."

"Ah, yes, Roswell—your answer to everything." Harlan shook his head. Maybe this alien's trip had somehow rearranged his alien marbles, assuming, of course, that he'd had any to begin with. He pushed the elevator button for the lowest level.

Five minutes later, "87" flashed in bright green LED lights and the elevator opened into a long, dark, concrete corridor. Red lights, dim, flashed along the walls, creating just enough illumination for Harlan to see where he was going. But before leaving the elevator he pressed HOLD to ensure that he could get out of this modern dungeon.

Walking with gazelle-like steps, the alien made its way to the hallway's end. A door, metal reinforced with iron, blocked the way.

"Earthling, here."

When Harlan caught up, he noticed twin locks in the door.

"Can you open it, Earthling?"

He looked up, disbelieving, into the white eyes. "Open it?! Are you kidding me? No. I'd need the key—can't you?"

"We are not a violent race," the alien said in hushed tones. "But if *you* would use this," one three-fingered hand held up a white object, elongated with several wires protruding from one end and a trigger underneath.

Harlan chuckled to himself as he took the thing and held it. "You had this the whole time?" When the alien did not reply but merely gestured at the sealed door, Harlan chuckled again. "A ray gun . . . you have got to be joking."

Pulling the trigger unleashed a bolt of energy, blasting a large hole in the door's locking mechanisms. Pocketing the ray gun, Harlan kicked the door, swinging it into the room beyond.

There, lying under a polymer dome, was an alien identical to the first one.

"Roswell!" the first alien said. It lifted the dome and laid its hand on the prone figure. The green glove glowed with green light, the alien under the dome rose from the medical (or experimental) table and warbled at his rescuer.

"Earthling, Roswell says thank you."

Harlan arched his brows. "*This* is Roswell? But I thought Roswell was a ship?" He scratched his head, chuckling. "So this is your?"

"In Earth terms: Roswell is my cousin."

Roswell stood, thin legs shaking. His green head, devoid of a helmet, showed bald beneath the harsh florescent lights in the room. "How can we repay the Earthling?"

The first alien cocked his head to the side, white eyes returning Harlan's stare. "This Earthling has enemies. They would like him dead."

"But he saved me. Led you here," Roswell replied.

Both aliens spoke in unison. "What reward, Earthling? What reward do you desire?"

A smile spread across Harlan's face and he snapped his fingers. He knew exactly what he wanted.

The flying saucer hovered for a few minutes above the desert, above Area 51, then it climbed above Earth's atmosphere. Harlan, pinned between his newfound friends, looked down at the planet. He hadn't seen much of it, only bits and pieces, but a trip to another world was an opportunity this Earthling wasn't willing to pass up.

The little ship raced away from the planet, the blue planetary jewel, Earth, receded from until Harlan could have held it in his hand. Space streamed around him, spiraled, dizzying fast. He tapped his oversized helmet and smiled.

So long, Victor Bell!

COMET'S PASSAGE

Upon a silver horse, Comet rode through the sky
His mount's hair flying up, around, behind him,
In glorious, cascading light

The likes of which
The world beneath him
        Had never seen.

He urged on his powerful, space charger
Charting his course to the left, around, behind the planet,
Exulting, soaring beyond

Until the world below him,
Was the world behind him,
        And he moved on.

The stars dimmed, acknowledging his superior light
And his charger dropped silvery hairs glowing, burning,
    in its wake,
A trail of fire fading, dimming

So that the world behind
And the stars they passed
        Would not soon forget.

To other planets, Comet journeyed
Guiding his horse between, above, beyond
Through cold space, streaming

He wheeled his beast,
To re-enter the solar system,
        The familiar cycle to repeat.

ABACUS ONE

The deck plates of Abacus One vibrated as it shot through the nebula. *Riding the great waves of space.* The panel above Charles' head flashed green and the cockpit control panel lit up with every color of a rainbow. But it had been a long, long time since he'd seen a rainbow . . . since his feet had rested on a planet's surface instead of the cozy confines of his ship. Ah, but he loved this vessel and the mission for which he now purposed her.

His communications panel blipped and then crackled with static. He heaved a sigh and smiled as the enforcer spoke. "Unidentified craft, this Space is restricted. Reverse heading, otherwise we will open fire."

The orange and blue gases of the nebula streamed around the Abacus One as it pierced a veil of red haze and emerged in open space. An earth-like planet orbited an orange star in his forward window. Glowing specks floated around the planet and in the space between it and his ship.

"Unidentified craft, respond." Three torpedo ships angled away from the planet and approached him. Their silver hulls reflected the vivid colors of the nebula, the planet, and the star.

God, I pray, be with me and see me through this. Charles keyed the controls and sat back in his leather command chair. The Abacus One trembled as her engines engaged at full burn.

His small, narrow hull cut between the enforcers' whale ships, dispersing clouds of glowing dust. The enforcers opened fire in a blur of heated projectiles the size of his headrest. Trails of flaming orange cloud indicated the trajectory of each missile. The planet grew in his viewport, silent and beautiful . . . but the projectiles would reach him before he reached it.

He swallowed, glanced at the green button overhead, then folded his hands over his face. *If I do this, Lord, it may be the last thing I do.* As the enforcers' missiles trailed within a thousand feet of Abacus One's black hull, he pulled a digital reading pad from his pocket. As it flashed on he read, "'Go ye into all the world and preach the gospel to every creature.'"

Setting down the pad, he leaned forward, moving his practiced fingers over the navigation panel. The Abacus One groaned to the side, rolled left, then banked toward the planet's atmosphere. He glanced sidewise through the smaller viewport. The enforcers' ships shrank behind him as the planet's gravity thrust him forward, but the missiles—spread as they were like flies in the wind—tightened into formation, turning with greater speed than his ship was capable.

Well, he'd come this far not to fail.

As the planet turned closer to him and filled the cockpit viewports ahead and to the side, he stood and folded his arms behind his back. Snaking ribbons of blue interspersed with vast deserts on the planet below. Yet four green continents stared back at him. Colonized over three hundred years ago when interstellar travel first became possible, the planet had broken ties with its home world. Disastrous. But now the time had come to deliver a message, a message of hope and a promise of peace to a cut-off people.

The enforcers' missiles hammered the Abacus One's hull, deadly harbingers of death. But he calmly stepped up to the green button, reached up, and pressed it with a smile as a missile exploded against the cockpit and space burned the air from his lungs.

The belly of Abacus One opened as the hull buckled under multiple small explosions. The nose and cockpit twisted, flames spitting into space, even as a million metallic orbs emptied from Abacus One's belly. The enforcers' ships grew larger, approaching their prey. But the metallic orbs fell toward the planet's atmosphere.

Nina clapped her little hands and giggled atop her father's shoulders, and he bounced her. The green fields and orange trees spread around them as far as the eye could see, and his round house lay a quarter mile away. He wondered in that brief moment what his ancestors had seen when they walked on Earth. And what was their history? To him such knowledge had been lost. Ten elders ruled these United Continents, yet they forbid anything taken from the old world. No customs were to be followed, no gods to be worshipped, and no code of conduct save that which the elders deemed appropriate.

He glanced at the night sky. Orange and blue nebulous clouds bloomed in the heavens and a few dozen stars twinkled rapidly. According to some people, back on the home world you could see billions of stars on a dark night. He could only imagine what that would be like.

Then something happened that had never happened in the many nights he'd walked out of doors. A new star radiated into existence, then died out, and a million lesser stars fell from the sky. They burned brilliant trails in every direction as if stretching to every corner of his world . . . and one crashed into the field a thousand feet from where he stood. It kicked up a cloud of dirt and dust.

As the dust settled a crater appeared. He set Nina on her feet and, holding her hand, walked over the rim. There, glowing white-hot, lay a metallic sphere which cooled with surprising speed. Moisture steamed from it and cracks webbed around its smooth surface. Then it broke into many tiny fragments and something thin and white unrolled from its interior.

With trembling fingers he reached out, knelt, and unraveled the paper and read "God's story" from the top. As he read the text that followed something deep in his heart stirred and he opened his mind to the Christ who died for his sins.

Above the planet the remnants of Abacus One rolled through space. Captain Charles' body could not be found, but his errand of truth—like that of countless missionaries before him—planted the seed of God's love where man had sought to destroy it.

MOSES AND THE LAMB

There was long ago a little lamb who was owned by a young Israelite boy named Jacek. The lamb was white as fallen snow and loved its master. Jacek and his parents had left the land of Egypt because God had told them through his prophet, Moses.

One night the lamb overheard Jacek speaking with his mother.

"Son," Jacek's mother said. "You were touching the animals again. Have you washed your hands?"

Jacek smiled up at her. "Yes, Mother. My hands are washed."

But the little lamb had been following Jacek all day, as it often did. It knew that Jacek had not washed his hands. Jacek had lied.

Jacek walked over to his bed and lay down as if to take a nap. But he tossed and turned in his bed.

The little lamb hung its head and walked out of Jacek's family's tent. It bleated as it walked the dusty path between the tents and marched up to the largest tent of all, the Tabernacle where the people worshipped God.

As it stepped up to the tabernacle Moses strode out and looked at the sky. His skin had been darkened by the sun and he was dressed quite tall. His sandaled foot touched the lamb's leg and it bleated up at him.

With a sigh and a gentle shake of his head, Moses knelt and patted the lamb's soft head. "Are you lost, little fellow?" He looked over the lamb at the many tents pitched around the tabernacle. "I wonder where your flock is," Moses said.

Moses stood again and started to walk past the lamb, but it bleated and stepped in front of his sandaled feet, looking up at him. It wanted to speak to this man but all it could do was bleat.

Suddenly a man appeared beside Moses. He wore a glowing white robe and his strong face shone with holy light. The man smiled down at the lamb and said, "Stand still, Moses, for I am an angel sent from God."

Moses stepped back.

The angel leaned over the lamb and said, "God has regard for even the smallest of his creations, Moses. He cares for you, he cares for his people, he cares for the birds of the air, and he cares for lambs such as this one. This night a soul will find its way to the Lord. This night God has given this lamb a voice to speak. And you, His prophet, will hear the words of one of His gentlest creatures."

Kneeling in front of the lamb, the angel kissed its tiny forehead. Then he walked off into the tents of Israel. Soon the tall, shining figure vanished into thin air.

Moses knelt on the ground. He rubbed his hands over his tired, aging legs, and the lamb gazed into his eyes. "Prophet of God, please hear me," it said in one of the gentlest voices Moses had ever heard. It was almost too gentle, too soft to be heard.

"Speak, little lamb, and I will listen."

"I am the companion of a very young Israelite whom I love dearly. He cares for me with all the love in his heart. But tonight I heard my young master lie to his mother. It was not a big lie, great prophet, but

Moses and the Lamb

I fear that the first sin, once committed, hardens his young heart. And his next sin will be greater."

Tears sprang into the lamb's round, black eyes. "Great prophet, I have come to you this night because I do not want this first sin to open the way for greater sins that will condemn him to eternal death."

"What is it you want of me?" Moses asked. He reached out and held the little lamb's chin with his fingers.

The little lamb said, "I wish to amend the boy's sin in the sight of God."

"Where is your young master?" Moses asked.

"He tosses and turns in his bed while he lays in his father's tent. The battle between his conscience and his flesh . . . is being waged." A tear slipped out of the lamb's eye, soaking into the wool under its eye. "Will you help me do this, mighty prophet?"

Moses smiled as the tears welled in his own eyes. "Let it be as God has decreed in his commandments, little lamb. But only promise me this: that the boy will come and bear witness."

"No, no I could not bear to have it so." But the lamb stopped shaking its head and started walking toward the tents. "As you command, Moses, I will bring him."

"Then," Moses stood and sighed, "I will consult the Lord and prepare for your return."

Jacek was sitting on his bed when the little lamb returned to the tent. It walked up to him, nudged him with its tiny hoof, and asked him to follow it outside. Jacek was very surprised to hear his lamb speak, so surprised that he stood and followed it out of the tent. It led him down the rows of tents all the way to the great tabernacle.

There, in the darkness, stood the prophet of God. Jacek had never been so close to the former prince of Egypt. He gazed at the man in awe, thinking again that this was a very strange dream.

Moses reached down and lifted Jacek's lamb off of the ground and stood it on the altar. "In payment for your sin, son of Israel," Moses said, drawing out a long knife that glistened in the starlight, "innocent blood must be spilled so that God's justice is satisfied."

Without fighting and without a sound, the little lamb lay on its side and turned its black eyes sadly toward Jacek. "Remember this night whenever you lie again," it said.

Jacek ran forward to stop Moses. "It was my lie! It was my sin!"

He tripped on a rough stone and fell flat on his face. When he pulled himself up, he brought his hand away from his throbbing nose. Blood stained his fingers crimson. And then he knew: this was not a dream.

"Wait!" he cried.

But the blade glistened in the starlight as it slit the lamb's throat. The blood flowed onto the altar and the little white lamb's eyes paled from black to gray.

Trembling as the shock and reality of the sacrifice sank into his young mind, Jacek knelt and wept. Over and over he whispered, "How? How did my little lie cause this?"

Moses's large hand held his shoulder. Jacek looked up into the prophet's eyes. A blade dripping blood was in the prophet's other hand.

"If you listen to me, Jacek, then I will tell you of the God of our fathers." Moses squeezed Jacek's shoulder firmly. "Let me lead you to the Lord of mercy and love. Let me lead you to the just and holy God. If you follow God then this sacrifice will not have been in vain."

That night the little lamb walked into heaven's green fields. Angels ran to meet it with smiles on their faces. They sang praises to God that, because of the little lamb's sacrifice, Jacek had learned the penalty of sin. And that night they greeted the little lamb and touched the scar across its throat. The green fields free of sin and lit by the glory of God, the eternal lands of the Creator, spilled forth an abundance of creatures and people smiling, laughing, praising God. And the little lamb joined them.

THE FAITHFUL FEW

The fight had hardly begun and we pulled back,
Afraid of being injured by the darts of the wicked.
Our sin-bearer cried out from his cross,
"Why have you stopped? I have given the battle to you."

But we fell back under each new wave of temptations,
We held up our white flags, "Truce! We cannot overcome!"
The enemy broke through our ranks, that wicked serpent,
And laughed the savior to scorn.

A few of our number, with tears in their eyes,
Cried out to the Savior, "Lord, forgive us!"
And he looked upon them with favor and forgave them.
"Now go forth! Through me you have overcome."

We watched the faithful drive into the enemy ranks,
Taking punishment from the enemy that we had not seen.
But though they cringed and faltered, the faithful pressed on.
Their blood flowed freely and they drew the serpent's blood
    in return.

"Come, Christians," the serpent told us,
"Watch and see the opposition. Is it worth your lives?
These men and women that come against me
Will fall into the greatest of trials."

But the faithful few fought on, drawing nigh to the cross.
The serpent sent his minions against them
And the battle grew fiercer than before
And the darts of the wicked drove us farther back.

"Draw back!" we told the faithful few.
"He is too strong, you will die!"
"Is it better to die in the service of our Lord," replied they,
"Or to give in to temptation, and never to fight?"

Temptations rained thick and fast upon us
Until it seemed that we had joined the enemy ranks
And we practiced warfare in the manner of the serpent,
Using guile, instead of truth.

When at last we looked again upon the cross
We saw the faithful few, dead at its base,
Their blood pooling beneath the Savior
And his tears raining down upon their bodies.

The Faithful Few

"See then how great is their loss?" the serpent asked.
"Had you stood by them the same fate would be yours.
Now you are like me, in thought and deed,
Yielders to sin, and traitors, beyond redemption."

But the Savior cried that the serpent had lost
And the faithful dead rose around his feet.
He stepped down from the cross
And we saw that he had suffered willingly.

The faithful few were robed in white
The Savior gave to each of them a gold crown
And he gave them a new song to sing:
A song of victory that crushed the serpent's host.

When the Serpent had been destroyed,
We wept at the Savior's feet.
He forgave us and clothed us with white,
But the crowns of gold we did not receive.

For whosoever will save his life shall lose it;
but whosoever shall lose his life for my sake
and the gospel's, the same shall save it.
–Mark 8:35 (KJV)

THE LITTLE CHILDREN COME

As the lion passed each little bed, he paused to look at the child sleeping there. The beds filled the room and the room was of enormous size.

"The serpents are on the move again, Horthan," the lion rumbled. "They will attack the village in the valley before night falls."

The tiger keeping pace beside him, sighed. "I have heard . . . Those villagers are a hard-hearted lot, full of endless questions, devoid of belief beyond what they can see with their eyes. Did they not kill the last prophet sent to them?"

The lion turned his shaggy head to look into the tiger's eyes. "As they killed the prophet before him. The message must be given if there is even a chance of redeeming their souls."

Horthan dipped his head toward the floor. "Then I will go. I will tell them myself."

"If they will not hear you, Horthan, then they have indeed fallen far. Go now, I will watch for your return."

The young woman's wild, innocent blue eyes pleaded with the people far more effectively than her words. She appealed to them, begged of them. "If we leave this village, passing outside the wall that encircles it, the serpents will kill us all!"

Standing with solemn demeanor in the midst of the crowding villagers, a large tiger spoke against her. "The serpents will not harm those who follow me, for I will protect them. Come forward, stand with me, *believe* in me. I can only give you this opportunity once.

"When you decide to stay, you choose death. Choose me and have life."

The young woman tore at her hair, causing several young men to move toward her and sooth her. "Can't you see?" she cried. "The tiger will lead us all to our deaths. You have seen the force surrounding this village . . . Can one animal protect us from such overwhelming odds?" She pointed a trembling, thin finger at the tiger. "If he is so certain of his promise, why doesn't he go out and destroy them instead of asking us to leave our homes?"

"The girl is right," one woman in the crowd said, looking up at the dark and stormy sky. "The tiger's promise sounds good but he offers no proof of his ability to carry out that promise."

"I am only the messenger," the tiger replied. "But you know for Whom I speak."

"And does the mighty lion really care what happens to us," the young woman screamed. "He lives in power, afraid of nothing, yet he lets us suffer." Her eyes burned into the crowd and her hands touched the young men's faces. "The serpents are here *because* of the lion. We should surrender now, while we still can. After all," she took a moment to wipe tears from her face, "if we surrender, the serpents have promised us peace. What more can we ask?"

Murmurs of consent raced through the crowd like wildfire. The village leader's boot ground the gravel as he stepped toward the tiger and pointed his finger at it. "You are not welcome here, Horthan! Go now and leave us in peace. We will not follow you."

But Horthan's eyes had found a child in the crowd, a little girl. The little girl stared back at him for a long moment, a moment during which the village leader and those encircling Horthan, including the young woman, turned their attention to the young one.

Without warning, the child broke free of its mother's hand. Ignoring her scream, it raced to Horthan and wrapped its arms around his neck. "B-believe. I believe," she said. Squinting her eyes shut in response to the abusive language now coming from the villagers' mouths, the little girl clung to the tiger, her blond curls blowing gently in a hot breeze.

Horthan enveloped the innocent one in his furry arms and covered her head with his paws, knowing what would come next. The villagers, led by the young woman, picked up the nearest hard object they could grab hold of, and cast them at the child. But Horthan took the blows instead and the little girl was unharmed. Bricks bruised his ribs, stones cut his hide until blood began to flow, but he smiled in spite of it, feeling only the little one's arms around his neck.

With a roar and a flashing of his razor claws, Horthan drove the villagers back. Then he helped the child onto his back. "Hang on to me tight, young one." Racing through the startled villagers, he left the village via the main gate.

As he emerged into the land outside the walls, Horthan instructed the child to keep her eyes shut. Obediently, the child complied, burying her face in his scruff.

All manner of serpents maneuvered to attack the village. They were both large and small, scaled and not, venomous and fire-breathing (some were most definitely fully dragon) the dark, slimy creatures squirmed like a thousand worms and moved as if to attack him. The stink of them reminded him of broken, rotten eggs. He growled a warning and they, with evil eyes rebelling, slunk back, leaving him a clear path out of the battle zone.

The village was set in a small valley. When Horthan reached its rim and the first dragons threw flames, lighting the village walls like kindling, he did not bother to look back. Nor did he slow his pace when the serpents, large and small, sprang over the walls, looking for victims.

Back at the village, after the tiger departed, the village leader let out a long breath and turned to the young woman. "It's going to be all right," he said. "Horthan is gone. You were right . . . we just had to pick a side."

The young woman's pretty mouth opened in a laugh that, at first, sounded gleeful. Then it cracked and rose, cackling. Her legs melded together, black scales taking the place of cream skin. Her head elongated, teeth sharpening, mouth extending into a dragon's fearful jaws. Horns grew from her head and her hands stretched, closed into fists before reopening with leathery black skin between them. The leathery skin flexed with her arms, stretched to her sides and she rose before the village leader, disguise dropped.

Now in its true form, the inky black dragon ripped into the village leader's chest with its claws. As he died slowly in the dragon's fist, the village leader sputtered, "B-but we did as you asked . . . why do you not leave?" His trembling arm managed to point at the village's main gate. "Horthan . . . you've let him pass?"

"Fool," the dragon hissed. "Only in your last moments do you see that I am the Father of Lies, Ruler of Hell. I and mine have already fallen into darkness . . . all I want is to bring as many of your kind with me into eternal damnation as I can!"

With tooth and claw, the dragon hunted down the villagers. Those that it cornered, it sat back and let the flames pour from its mouth until their corpses were burned beyond recognition.

Horthan strode forward on all fours, claws clicking on the metal tiles of the path he followed. The path stretched on for as far as his tiger eyes could see through fields of waving green grass. He felt the child on his back dig a little harder with her knees to keep from falling off.

He thought of the hundreds of humans in the village from which the child came. They were still surrounded by masses of fire-breathing serpents. If the humans had only listened to him and followed him through the gap in the enemy lines. He had the right of passage. No servant of wickedness could harm him, for they feared his master.

Being careful not to dump his precious cargo, Horthan looked back. It seemed that his vision extended all the way back to the village. The winged serpents roiled about the village perimeter. They slipped their long, forked tongues like whips among the screaming mass of humanity. Flames leaped from their maws and they lashed out with claws and teeth, wreaking havoc, reaping blood.

Horthan turned away and trod the path with a heavy heart. But the little girl stroked his fur and leaned down, wrapping her arms around his neck. "Do not worry, Child. I am not going to leave you behind," he said.

Just then the land behind him began to teem with the hoards of murderous serpents. Having finished with the village they were after new blood. Some of them spread their leathern wings and shot through the air. They circled above him, waiting as the others dug into the earth as they ran, trying to overtake him.

"Hold on tight, Child," Horthan started to run. With powerful strides he ate the trail, hearing the hungry growls of his enemies on his heels. At first they were only behind him. Then they closed in from both sides of the trail.

The green grass was torn from the ground, other serpents' heads ripping through from under the dirt they'd concealed themselves in. They grabbed at the child, struck at Horthan. But the way ahead was still open to him and now a mountain arose at the path's end.

A gate at the mountain's base opened to receive him. He could see the blinding golden light of the lion king as it waited for him.

The serpents must have realized they were losing their chance to strike. Horthan heard flames shoot from overhead and beside him. The metal tiles of the path melted under intense heat, burning away the hair on his paws and blistering his feet.

Just in time, he saw a dragon dive, claws groping for the child. Horthan reached the little girl first, coming to a sudden stop with his bleeding feet painting a red trail behind him. The serpent's claws struck mere seconds after he pulled the child from his back and clutched her in his arm. Like hooks catching in his back, the dragon's claws ripped into Horthan and pulled away his flesh. The pain stabbed through him with such force that his heart ceased to beat.

With the last ounce of energy he had, Horthan threw the child toward the gate and the lion. Like vultures finishing wounded prey, the dragons dug into him. His striped hide was torn, his ears ripped like leaves.

As his vision darkened, Horthan smiled. He saw the little girl standing inside the gates. Beside her, in blinding glory, the lion rose as guard. The few serpents that dared fly through the gates met quick deaths. For beams of light shot from the lion's eyes, beams that cut out their hearts.

The Little Children Come

In the child's eyes, Horthan saw tears and a new light of understanding. Tears of sorrow for its deliverer coupled with an awe for the ultimate sacrifice he was willingly making.

Death came quickly after that.

The lion woke Horthan with a roar of victory.

Horthan rolled off the straw-covered table and flexed his strong arms, dug his claws into the stone floor. Then he reached around to his back and felt the deep scars from the dragon's claws.

"Well done, Horthan," the lion said. "Well done."

"But I could not save the others," Horthan looked over at a cot in the golden chamber. On it lay the child, safe at last and forever. "They doubted me," he said of the others. "If they had followed me out of the village they would have been saved. But they debated science and religion, and refused to place their faith in me. They worried that the serpents would kill them if they left the village. I had no choice but to give them up . . . in order that I might save this one."

"Ah," the lion stepped up to the cot and his mane streamed behind him. "The faith of a child . . . marvelous isn't it? It is always the little ones who hear your call. It is always they who are able to shed doubt in order to follow the light."

"Yes," Horthan reached out with his paw and gently stroked the child's head. "The little children come to me."

CARRIAGE ANGEL

The temptation to slam the door behind him almost won out. Francis shook his head and grasped the brass knob. With a firm but gentle hand he closed the door and walked down the long, arched hallway. The buzz of indiscernible conversations from fellow college students drove him out of the building into pouring rain.

Up and down the street he glanced until a black carriage rolled his way and the driver slowed his horses. "Need a ride, son?"

"Surely I do." He sighed, opened the carriage door, and stepped in. The contraption bounced under his weight and he closed his eyes, listening to the driver cluck to the horses. The clopping of hooves dipped in and out with the wheels rolling over cobblestones and the pattering rain.

"Where to, son?" the driver asked.

Francis exhaled and opened his eyes. It was then he saw her. Her skin was the softest olive he'd ever laid eyes on. Though her eyes were closed in sleep, he imagined them ocean storm grey. Her fingers thin and long . . . she must have played a piano. But beside all this she wore a soft yellow dress with a white lace bonnet. While all around him lay dimness—the evening rain and the dark carriage interior complete with black leather seats—she rested like a spring flower at dawn.

The driver's seat creaked as the man leaned closer to the carriage window to say, "Young man. Where shall I take you?"

Home, he could have easily said it. Yet as he leaned into the opposite corner from her the school board master's harsh words lost their potency.

"Reginald Peters is a good student, yes. But unless you can pay his tuition on top of your own . . . we have no choice save to drop him from this institute."

"But, sir," he'd said. "Surely his need is great. Surely you can see that. This institute can keep him on without suffering financially and there is no friend so faithful as he."

"Young Francis," the master had shaken his head. "Your tuition was paid up front, in full, by your parents. We do not run a charity for unfortunate fellows, neither do we shun them. But unless their tuition and board is paid, like yours, they must be expelled."

As the carriage bounced, Francis glanced over the young woman's face. Peace and solitude, freedom and companionship. Why did she remind him of these things?

He leaned his head out the carriage window, lest he disturb her. "Here is enough for the night's ride, I think. If you don't mind I'll just ride for a while."

"Need a place to think, eh?"

"Will that be sufficient cash?"

The man nodded. The carriage rolled on down the streets of the city. The gas lanterns stood at every corner and at points between along the sidewalks. Iron guardians of the night, illuminating the water runs along the cobblestones and in front of the shops and homes he passed.

All along his mind passed from the costly education he did not desire and the stranger sleeping in the carriage. The carriage jarred her and he reached forward, gently holding her shoulder so that she did not fall. She stirred and he withdrew to the dark recesses of the carriage. As she opened her eyes a lamp flashed by the window. Her eyes were green, a lovely green. But she closed them, sinking back against the carriage cushion.

It would have been relaxing to cross to her side and put his arm around her so she could rest her head on his shoulder. But what man would do a fool thing like that for a strange woman? Not he, that was certain. He shook his head, admiring the curves of her face until he almost blushed.

As an hour wore by another passenger halted the carriage. "Percy Street, driver." A lanky fellow brushed passed him and turned to sit next to her and his elbow narrowly missed her head.

Pressing his finger to his lips, Francis pulled the man to sit beside him. "Why, what do you—"

But Francis shook his head and his gaze flicked back to her. The new arrival leaned forward, reached out for her shoulder as if to wake her. With a slap to the knuckles, Francis caused the fellow's hand to retreat. In silence they rode on and she never stirred.

The carriage rolled to a stop outside a tavern and a burly man teetered inside. He glanced from one side to the other, burped with liquor breath, and with a sober face he sat between Francis and the other fellow, eyes fixated on the young woman. The carriage lurched forward.

None of the passengers said a word but the two men beside him smiled and doffed their hats when the maiden opened her eyes. She straightened in the seat and the drunk burped. She shook her head with such depth of sorrow that Francis felt a lump form in his throat. The drunk nodded at her and hung his head. Her hand touched his cheek and sympathy passed over her countenance as she pressed a small black book into his hand.

The next stop, the drunk stepped out. He opened the little book under a lamp, squinting at the first pages. But the carriage shot down the street and the young woman settled back into her corner with her head lolled sideways.

Not long afterward the carriage stopped again and the other fellow got out, casting a last glance at her as the carriage left him standing in the rain.

For a long while Francis watched her sleep, then he leaned out the carriage window. "Driver, return me to the institute."

"Certainly, young man. Certainly." The horses plodded down a side street and before long the carriage rolled to a stop in front of the institute. "Wait here, driver."

He sloshed up the steps and knocked. A butler answered, let him inside, and he followed the hallway back to the school master's office.

"Ah, a pleasure to see you again, Master Francis." The man laughed and stood from his leather chair. The broad mahogany desk danced with flickering light from the fireplace.

"Sir," Francis smiled, "the journey I took to this institute was not of my own choosing. It was, rather, a decision made by others in my stead. But here I stand, having a free education for which I care not. No disrespect intended, Head Master. The merits of this institute speak for themselves, but this is not the place for me."

"What?" The man stepped back. "But it is already paid for. What an opportunity you have been given! Do not take it lightly."

"I don't, and that is why I have decided to request that the funding for my education be, instead, given to Reginald Peters. For he is deserving and will proudly succeed in his studies."

The man shook his head. "It is not so simple as that, young man. One cannot simply tell the institute to transfer the balance of your tuition to Mr. Peters' account—"

"No, I am certain you are right. It will not be simple, yet it is the right thing to do." Francis shook the man's hand and smiled. "I will be back in the morning to sign all the necessary papers."

Francis left the institute. The rain pelted his face as he stepped up the carriage. "I will ride a while longer. Please drive on."

Until past the midnight hour he rode in the carriage. But his only companion was her.

When the town clock struck the hour, she opened her eyes and seemed to notice him for the first time.

"This is where you get off, Miss Mary." The driver pulled the carriage to a stop in front of a brick-fronted home with an ornate iron fence around it. Warm light glowed from one large window on the first floor and a man inside gazed down at the carriage.

Francis pulled his attention back into the carriage. Her green eyes stared back at him as she gathered her dress, and Francis opened the carriage door, stepping into the rain. He held the door and proffered his hand. Light as a dancer she touched his hand and lowered herself to the pavement.

The house door opened and a man bustled forth, holding an umbrella. "Mary, come inside. Your mother is worried for you."

Francis kissed the hand. It was only a quick kiss, but he glanced into her eyes before she turned to her father.

The man kissed her forehead and smiled down at Francis. "It gives me comfort to see a gentleman is also up at this hour." Then, turning to Mary, he said, "Will you introduce me to this young fellow?"

She lowered her gaze and color mounted her cheeks.

"Oh! This is the first time you've met?" The man eyed Francis and for a moment he expected criticism. But her father laughed.

"Come back tomorrow for luncheon and we'll become acquainted. My daughter will cook you the finest meal in this city and afterward . . . well, what do you say?"

With a meaningful bow, Francis thanked the man and glanced meaningfully into *her* eyes. "I will be there."

"Splendid! Now, come my daughter. You need sleep."

Father and daughter turned toward the house and entered. Francis stood on the sidewalk as she closed the door. Then he stepped up the carriage and found the driver staring after the girl. "She rides in my carriage many nights. She says nothing, only offers her sweet smile. There have been times when poorer people cannot come up with the fare, but her sweet hand dug into her purse and made up the difference. Other times I've seen her give that little book to perfect strangers and the same strangers become God-fearing, solid people." The driver smiled broadly. "Young man, you met an angel tonight."

THE GATES OF BLISS

In the dull monotony of my life nothing ever changed. I woke with the dawn and left for the office after a bowl of cereal and a bagel, worked through the day, and returned home to my lonely apartment. At twenty-five-years-old I had all-but-given-up on relationships, my last one having ended with *her* going off with another man. Financially I was doing ok. I paid the bills and even saved some money for retirement, yet something was always missing and I knew what it was: a sense of purpose, that drive to keep me going. All this finally seemed to come to an end on the night that I received the phone call.

"Hello?" I said.

"Hi," a male voice answered. "Is this Herbert?"

"Yes. Who's this?"

"No one in particular."

This was a strange answer. I held the phone away from my ear and eyed it, considering the consequences of severing the connection and leaving No One In Particular to find another victim. But since my day had been as dull as all the others I decided to converse with my anonymous caller.

"Ok, Mr. No One In Particular. Why did you call?"

"No special reason."

No special reason? What kind of nut is this guy?

"Why did *you* pick up?"

His question left me puzzling over my own motives for a minute until I finally answered: "I don't know."

"Were you bored?"

"Maybe." I was beginning to talk like him now, with each sentence indefinite.

The fellow cleared his throat. "And you are doing nothing now?"

"I am talking to you."

"About what?"

"Nothing. I guess." If he kept this up I'd soon lose my patience and hang up, but his next words caught my interest.

"Good, then get in your car and leave with no destination in mind."

"Why?"

"You don't need to know. In fact it is better if you do it for no reason at all." There was a click on the other end and the number disconnected.

Checking my Caller I.D. I was startled to read. "Mr. No One In Particular." Beneath that, where the phone number should have been, the screen was blank. It was as though the call from Mr. No One In Particular came from nowhere.

Now I had a decision to make: do as my mysterious caller had said, or stay here and continue in my boredom. *But why should I go? I have no reason . . . . Is that good?* Thinking that it probably was I left with nothing except my clothes, wallet, a watch, and my keys. Revving the engine of my '89 Firebird lifted my spirits. The day was partly cloudy and slivers of sunlight illuminated the road ahead.

I drove out of town in no definite direction, feeling rather foolish as I turned onto random roads and found myself several times in the same location, having gone in circles. Yet there was something wholly natural to this endeavor and, even though you can probably not understand why, I felt pleased with myself for taking Mr. No One In Particular's advice—that is, for a time.

Then it occurred to me that the landscape had transformed around me and no longer did I recognize the road on which I traveled, the twisted trees that bordered it, or the clear sky with a red sun. *What have I done?* I pulled over to the roadside, put my car in neutral, engaged the emergency brake, and stepped outside.

Hardly a moment was allowed for me to breath in the clean, warm air. A motorcycle careened around a bend in the road ahead and struck a stone, sending its leather-dressed rider hurtling through the air to skid along the ground. I rushed forward to offer assistance and turned over the victim.

A grizzled-haired man smiled up at me and stood up. "Whew! That was a close call . . .. Thank you, friend, you saved my life." Before I could point out that he had not been injured by his fall, he ran down the road, righted his bike, and sped past me with a careless wave of his hand.

As I turned to get back in my car I heard a woman's scream from somewhere in the trees. I raced in the sound's direction until I came to a path in the woods. A young lady, no older than I, danced ahead of me. "Wait!" I called. "I heard someone scream . . .."

She spun around and smiled in a childish way. "Haw, haw, that was me!"

"Are you all right?"

"I think so."

"Then," I placed my hands on my hips, "why did you scream?"

She shrugged and walked off. "I had no particular reason."

What is wrong with her? What is this place? Why am I here? I raced back in a panic to my Firebird and drove further down the road. Shapeless houses and contorted shrubs lined the way and when I decided to ask for directions back home I could not get a satisfactory answer from the populace.

"You are nowhere, and in no place. You are here."

"But if you call it 'here' then it *is* a place and I *am* somewhere."

The fellow to whom I was talking seemed none too helpful and so I drove on until I found an old woman walking in circles in a yard. "Please, dear lady, can you tell me how to get home?"

"No." She winked at me. "For that would be someplace and this is nowhere, thus it is no place. How do you expect to get from nowhere to somewhere and from no place to a particular place? It is impossible and unnecessary. So settle down, young man. Relax and accept your fate: you will soon be one of us."

"And who would I be if I became one of you?" I asked with a decided note of sarcasm.

"A Nobody! We are all nobody and we, like you, used to be somebody, though now we cannot know who we were." She laughed. "Isn't it marvelous? And none of this would have been possible if we hadn't received the summons."

"The 'summons?'"

The old woman danced a jig and clapped her hands. "Surely you remember the summons. I received mine from Mr. Nobody an indefinite time ago."

Ah! At last I have a connection! Trying to hide the urgency in my voice (for I was desperate to depart this place and return to the normal world—where I was certain my perspective on life would never be the same) I posed the all-important question, my last hope. "Where might I find Mr. No One In Particular?"

Suddenly her eyes filled with suspicion and I suspected she had an inkling of my plan. So when she hit me with the question I feigned insult. "Why? You wouldn't be trying to get somewhere, would you?"

"Maam! I would never! I only want to thank Mr. No One In Particular for his phone call." This was not a lie, though if she'd guessed the *kind* of thanks I longed to deliver she would have held her tongue.

With a smug face she pointed me in the direction of Mr. No One In Particular who lived next to Mr. Nobody and Dr. Indecision. "I am glad for your sake that you have decided to stay with us," she said. "The guardians of Bliss would have punished you severely—you have such a cute face."

I burned rubber all the way to Mr. No One In Particular's house, passing the homes of Mrs. Nonsense and Ms. Do As I Please on the way. It was peculiar how only these houses (all situated on a hill overlooking the land of—I presume—Bliss) had people with unique, albeit peculiar, names. The others I'd met did not call themselves by *any* name. They were Nobodies. *How disturbing! They have lost the desire to be more than they are; they are complacent.*

Mr. No One In Particular answered my knock and, with one eye scrutinizing my Firebird, showed me in. "Welcome to Bliss, Nobody," he said in a jovial way, "where the ultimate condition of mankind is realized."

"And *what,* Sir, do you consider the ultimate condition of mankind?"

"Freedom, of course. You are now free from responsibility, free from care, free from moral judgment, and free to do as you please, anytime that you please. You have taken the first step into a new world, a world wherein God's laws no longer matter; a world of bliss! Welcome, I say, welcome!"

"Look," I said to him, pointing my finger at his face, "I didn't ask to come here and I don't want to be here . . . ."

He chuckled. "How wrong you are, Nobody, for you allowed your life to become a routine and you were comfortable, though unhappy with it. You see, in your world you are limited by conscience and human drive. Motivation is, for those in your world, a necessity imposed by the Creator. You try to be a better person, you dream of your future; you love the unlovable, and seek a life companion. Yet, in the end, this brings you nothing but misery.

"Despite your best efforts you still make mistakes every day, and as far as dreams are concerned only a few people achieve them. And what is it with giving your money to the poor and to other people you do not know; will they reward you with more money? No. They care only to get what you work so hard every year to earn."

Mr. No One In Particular scoffed, "Give up your desire for a wife. Why limit yourself by the bands of marriage when you could look around some more? The world is full of pleasures yet, as I said, your God-given conscience gets in the way of your desires. Thank goodness for the Land of Bliss! Here you can forget everything unpleasant and live for yourself."

"You mean until the judgment," I pointed out.

"If you say so, but then again: maybe that will never come."

I saw now what a fool I had been to listen to that pointless call and take this man's strange advice to go nowhere. *Herbert, you are a fool! Let's get out of here.* I had spoken and my conscience praised my decision while I shook my head at Mr. No One In Particular. "No, my destiny lies in the real world. I will not allow myself to grovel in self-absorption. Now, Sir, if you will be so kind as to show me the quickest way back to . . . .."

"Ha! You cannot leave, Nobody . . . ."

His manner of referring to me as one of the residents of Bliss was getting on my nerves. "*Stop calling me that!* I am Herbert, or don't you remember?"

THE GATES OF BLISS

"You cannot leave, *Herbert*. The guardians of Bliss will not permit it. You are stuck here—with us—until you become one of us."

Grabbing him by the shirt collar, I shook him as violently as I could. He was lightweight, like paper and I had no trouble rattling him around to make him tell me the truth. "All right—all r-right," he stammered. "Go on up the hill. The gates to your world are on the other side, yet I have told you the truth: the guardians will not permit you to pass."

"We'll see about that! And you had better not be lying to me . . .. If you are then I'll come back and, I can assure you, I will be in a sour mood."

On up the hill I drove, my reliable engine roaring all the way. On the other side I spotted the gates, just as my mysterious caller had told me and, guarding the gates, were two men dressed in black. They held machine guns—cocked at me and my beloved car—and the grins on their faces challenged me to get past them.

Two problems made themselves apparent to me: the men with the guns might kill me, and the gates were locked so that if I made a run for it there was no guarantee I would make it through. "You there," I called, sticking my head out the car window, "Pleasant day, don't you think?"

The answering rain of bullets forced me back into the car. The bullets shattered the windows, battered the hood, and tore up the seats. It was a miracle that none of them hit me. I left the car and ran back up the hill, trying not to let the guardians see the tears I was shedding for my car.

Back to Mr. No One In Particular I went and, when I had him, I dragged him up the hill and twisted his arm behind his back, forcing him to walk ahead of me. The guardians didn't fire again as I held my hostage before them and demanded that they open the gates. What a welcome sight greeted me as the heavy metal doors swung out and I saw the normal, partly cloudy skied world beyond.

Per my demands the guardians backed away from the gates, dropped their firearms, and pushed my battered vehicle through. I then released my prisoner and ran as hard as I could through the gates with the bullets nipping at my heels. I jumped into the Firebird, whooped with delight, and drove toward home. The gates of Bliss vanished behind me just as if they had never been there and I was safe.

"So long, Mr. No One In Particular. Next time you call . . . I'll hang up before I listen to another word of nonsense." *Now I know what my life was missing and I see where it was going. Never again will I allow myself to become complacent. This man is coming out of his shell!* My car sputtered and stalled. I got out, laughing at my former foolishness, and patted the Firebird's hood. "Wait here, my dear, I'll be back soon."

THE CONTRACT

There lived in a cottage by the sea a widow and her only child, a boy. He was a handsome lad, full of spirit and of an affable nature. To the widow her son was all in the world that mattered, and to her son she was all that mattered. But their estate was poor; their garden produced scant food and their purses held few coins.

One day the king of the sea (who was very rich and powerful) walked onto the beach by the poor widow's cottage and spoke to her son privately. "Give me ten years of servitude and I will give your mother ten years of wealth," he said. "She will neither want for anything and whatsoever she desires, that I will give to her."

"Very well," replied the lad. "We have an agreement."

The lad went to his mother and told her of his deal with the king of the sea. She wept and begged him not to go, but he said that he was bound to his word.

That night the king of the sea came to bring the lad to his palace beneath the sea. But the lad held up a hand to stop him. "First, we must sign three copies of our agreement so that neither of us can breach our contract."

The king of the sea laughed inwardly, for he thought to himself that it did not matter how many copies of an agreement he had signed so long as the lad came to serve him. "Once I have him in my underwater kingdom," the king reasoned, "he will not be able to escape from me and I will have him as my slave for eternity."

The king consented, and the lad called upon the goddess of the sea, the king of the birds, and the queen of all fairies as witnesses. Then he made three copies of the contract. One he drew upon the sand, one he wrote on paper, and one he etched into the face of a cliff.

The king of the sea thought to himself that this was quite humorous, because the lad copied their former agreement word for word in each location and signed them with the witnesses watching. "Now he will never be able to go anywhere in the world," thought he, "for he would break the contract." Thereupon, the king signed all three contracts and took the lad to his palace under the sea.

For three years the widow pined for her son and desired to have him back. So she wandered up and down by the sea until the king came up and she begged to be allowed to see the lad. "No," the king said. "He has not fulfilled the letter of his contract, and I have no intention of ever letting him go."

The widow, realizing the king's diabolical plan, wept sorely on the shore until her tears woke the goddess of the sea. "What is troubling you, good woman?" the goddess asked. "You are now wealthy beyond your dreams and healthier than you were three years ago."

"It is not for myself that I cry," the widow said. "My son is servant to the king of the sea, who has bound him under his word and will never let him go."

Furious to hear of the king of the sea's unjust conduct, the sea goddess called for the king of the birds, and the queen of the fairies.

Together they mulled over the problem and wondered how they could have been so blind to the king of the sea's plan. "We must right this matter," they said to one another, "for it is we who allowed the lad to go."

Finally, after much deliberation, they told the widow to go to the rock face and read the contract. "In it your son left the key to this problem," they said.

The widow did as they said and found the contract etched in the rock face. As she read, a smile crept to her lips and she began to dance and sing. "I know now, my son," she said. "I now know how truly wise your agreement with the king of the sea was."

Calling up the king of the sea, the widow told him to give her his crown and all that he had. "What?" he cried out in astonishment. "I will do no such thing!"

"Ah, but you must," the widow said. "I have read the contract and it says that whatsoever I desire of you will be given to me!"

The king of the sea made strong protest, but in the end the three witnesses forced him to live up to the letter of his contract and the widow became the queen of the sea. She made the king of the sea bring her to his underwater palace in his coral chariot, and there he made her queen over himself and all that he had and she made him her servant.

The widow's son was still bound by contract to serve the former king of the sea—though that man was now a servant also—but now he was treated well because his mother wore the crown. When the ten years had been completed, the son was free to depart and both he and his mother and all the inhabitants of the sea lived the rest of their lives in peace and prosperity.

THE SORCERESS AND THE MOUSE

In a house on a hill there once lived a sorceress of such extraordinary bad looks that no man would approach her. One night whilst she brooded over her misfortune, a mouse came to her door. "Tell me, Ms. Sorceress," said he, "If I could make men fall in love with thee: what, oh what would you give me?"

"Go away, little mouse," said the sorceress, "For if you continue to mock my condition I shall turn you into a worm!"

"Nay, I do not come to mock you," said he. "I am only a poor peddler and have come here with a potion to make your heart glad. Do not jump to conclusions about me, for I believe we may strike a mutually beneficial bargain."

The sorceress' ears itched to hear what more he had to say, but the mouse insisted that they speak where none could hear them. Thus, she closed her door and set down with the mouse in her parlor. It was a dusty room, full of cobwebs, spiders, and rotted wood.

"Now that I have brought you in, tell me what you have in mind," the sorceress demanded.

He stalled for a moment, twirled his whiskers and curled his tail. "I have been to the great wizard Merlin's residence," he began. "Of late the old man has taken to creating potions useless to himself but of great potential to others. One of those potions is the one I am prepared to offer thee . . . if the price is right."

Stomping her foot with impatience the sorceress leaned forward and said, "Linger no longer over words, little mouse; I have no patience for them. Tell me what I want to hear and I will give you all you require."

The little mouse thought to himself that this woman was a fool. For when one bargains they should never agree to any price. Rather they should bicker, barter, and reach the best deal. Nevertheless, he continued. "The potion I offer will grant you the love of any man your heart desires. All I ask in return is that you give me all your money and the money of those you ensnare with the potion."

To this the sorceress eagerly agreed and the bargain was struck. Then the mouse brought her the potion and, upon drinking it, she found that any man in whose eyes she looked was placed under a spell and did her bidding. Thus did she go to and fro through the village, stealing both the married and unmarried men and holding them captive to her will.

But the little mouse, who had himself gone through much trouble to procure the potion from the famed wizard Merlin, now found that the sorceress did not keep her end of the bargain. Instead she kept the money for herself and made herself wealthy.

So he went to the village and called a meeting with all the village women. "Hark!" said he, "It is I who can break the spell, but what can ye give me in return for my trouble?"

"Anything. Everything!" they rashly replied.

"Will ye make me your governor and be my servants, bring me whatever I desire, and do whatsoever I wish?"

"Yes, yes! If you can free our poor husbands than this we shall gladly do."

"Very well," said he. "Only remember this bargain and do not break your word or I will give the men back to the sorceress."

Then he took a mirror—which was as big as himself—and brought it to the sorceress' door. "Open up or I will take away that potion which I gave thee!" he cried.

"What a fool of a mouse!" thought she. "I have drunk the potion and he cannot take it back. I will now place him under the spell and he will also be my slave!"

As soon as she opened the door, the mouse closed his eyes and held up the mirror so that she cast the spell upon herself! Immediately the men were freed of the spell and returned to their homes.

It is said that to this very day, if you go the village wherein she lived, you will find her standing there still (though by now she has decayed to a mere skeleton). The villagers did not live up to their end of the bargain with the mouse and it is said of him that he returned to the aging wizard Merlin in hopes of finding revenge. But of such a thing I know not, for the little mouse was never heard from again.

ACKNOWLEDGMENTS

First I would like to thank my God and savior Jesus Christ. The stories in this book could not have been written had He not given me a healthy mind and body. I have sought to glorify Him in my writing and will continue to try and be the best Christian writer I can be. It is my desire to communicate truth, not simple stories.

Also I want to thank my fans for asking for a book like this. I've been mulling it over for a long while, but until recently did not have the necessary fan base to facilitate sales of an anthological work.

A special thank you goes to my wife, Kelley, and to Hannah Davis for proof reading *By Sword, By Right*. This project came in the midst of a crazy time in my life and their edits enabled me to polish this to my satisfaction.

TheSwordoftheDragon.com
FlamingPen.blogspot.com

Made in the USA
Middletown, DE
14 February 2025